Spy Another Day

SPY ANOTHER DAY

PHILIP CAVENEY

ANDERSEN PRESS • LONDON

First published in 2012 by
Andersen Press Limited
20 Vauxhall Bridge Road
London SW1V 2SA
www.andersenpress.co.uk

2 4 6 8 10 9 7 5 3 1

Copyright © Philip Caveney, 2012
British Library Cataloguing in Publication Data available.

ISBN 978 1 84939 417 8

Printed and bound by CPI Group (UK) Ltd,
Croydon, CR0 4YY

This one is for my two best girls...
Grace, who gave me the title,
and Susan, who gave me advice,
motivation and proofreading.

CHAPTER ONE

Saturday Matinee

Kip McCall let himself out of the house and walked into the village to his dad's cinema, the Paramount Picture Palace. It was a scruffy, single-screen cinema, one of the last of its kind in an age when multiplexes ruled. It was also a very special cinema. Since the arrival of its new projectionist, the mysterious Mr Lazarus, it could do something more than just show you the films – it could actually put you into them.

It was three months since Kip's adventure in the horror film, *Night on Terror Island,* and he had to admit that since then life seemed rather flat. That had happened during the summer holidays when he was spending all his spare time working at the Paramount. But now it was grey, miserable November; he was back at school and Mum had recently put her foot down, saying that homework was more important than helping his dad to sell popcorn and choc ices. In Kip's house, Mum's word was law.

Of course, he still met Beth at the pictures every Friday night so they could watch whatever new release was on offer – and today being Saturday, he was free to help out with the kids' matinee that always started at two p.m. Things weren't that bad...

But, still, why did everything seem so dismal? The main problem was that ever since his terrifying ordeal on the island, where he had been menaced by flesh-eating Neanderthals, giant snakes and a sabre-toothed tiger, Kip had found himself thinking wistfully about the experience. And, with each new film that came to the Paramount, he couldn't help wondering what it would be like to go into that film – to experience it *for real.* He knew it was crazy. He had come so close to being trapped in a monster movie for ever, doomed to do the same stupid things over and over again for the rest of his days... and yet... hadn't his visit to the island been the most incredible experience of his life? Wasn't there a tiny part of him that longed to repeat the it?

Mr Lazarus wasn't exactly helping. Every time he saw Kip he had that look in his cunning grey eyes... that, 'Ooh, Kip, see what we're showing *this* week!' kind of look. And Kip knew that the ancient projectionist was silently asking him if he would like to go to Baker Street to help Sherlock Holmes solve a crime ... If he would like to step into the arena to fight alongside a Roman gladiator ... If he fancied swinging on a rope with a horde of marauding pirates. Of course, he would have been a fool to go along with it because, when you went into a film, everything became real – real swords, real bullets, real monsters. He wasn't stupid enough to make that mistake a second time ... was he?

The Paramount came into view, looking a little less shabby than it had in the summer. Now audience figures were up, Dad had decided to use some of the extra money to give the building a bit of a makeover. He'd had the exterior sand-blasted, and he'd hired builders to replace some of the missing tiles – he'd even invested in a new lettering system, replacing the ancient black characters which went across the front of the canopy with shiny new ones in midnight-blue. Dad was also talking about getting the seats and carpets inside the building steam cleaned, something that hadn't been done in living memory.

Kip noticed a familiar figure standing on the steps of the picture house looking up at the COMING SOON! poster. It was Beth and she seemed lost in thought. Her short black hair was swept back from her face and her blue eyes were staring up at the poster entranced.

Beth was sort of Kip's girlfriend. Just before he'd left for Terror Island she had told him that she wasn't going to let 'her boyfriend' go on a dangerous mission alone. This had been news to Kip at the time; he hadn't realised that Beth thought of him as a boyfriend, but he'd taken it well. He liked her – the two of them were mates, had been for years – and, of course, they'd been hanging out with each other and going to the pictures together every Friday night for just about for ever – but since returning from the island nothing else had been said about the girlfriend–boyfriend thing. They had continued pretty much as before. Which Kip found kind of confusing. Weren't they supposed to be snogging by now? Only he couldn't bring himself to make a move like that in case Beth gave him a funny look and said, 'What do you think you're doing?' Which would be awful. So they were just kind of bumbling along as they always had.

As Kip came up to Beth, his gaze followed hers and came to rest on the poster for an upcoming film, *Spy Another Day*, the latest in the incredibly successful Jason Corder series. This explained Beth's enchanted expression. She liked the Corder films, just as lots of other people did, but she particularly liked Daniel Crag, the latest in a long line of good-looking actors to play the role of Agent Triple Zero. In fact, if Kip remembered correctly, Beth had once told him that Crag was 'seriously fit.' Whatever that meant.

So, little wonder she was gazing up at the image of the actor with such a faraway look on her face. Crag was dressed in a black tuxedo and he was cradling a huge gun in one hand, while his other arm was round the waist of an impossibly slim woman in a flimsy dress. Kip could imagine just what Beth was thinking. *What would it be like to go into that film and help Corder with his latest mission? What would it be like to meet Daniel Crag in the flesh?* Well, best to nip that one in the bud, he decided. He cleared his throat, a little louder than was strictly necessary.

Beth jumped and turned to look at him. Her cheeks reddened a little as though she realised that Kip knew exactly what was on her mind. She waved a hand at the poster. 'That, er . . . should be good,' she managed.

He frowned. 'The reviews are saying this might be Crag's last Corder film. He's done three now and they usually have a change after that.'

Beth looked shocked at the news. 'No way! He's the best Corder since Shane Connelly,' she said, referring to the man who had originally played the role back in the 1960s, and whose films were now only seen on TV on Sunday afternoons. Connelly's Corder had been suave and sophisticated – Crag had a different approach to the role; he was rough, hard, almost as nasty as the villains he fought, but a lot of females seemed to approve and Beth was no exception. She returned her attention to the poster. 'Can you imagine what it would be like to be in *Spy Another Day*?' she sighed.

Kip gave her a cold look. 'Forget it, Beth. Too dangerous.'

'Doesn't *have* to be. We could talk to Mr Lazarus, ask him to put us into a safe scene.'

Kip laughed at that. 'There's no such thing!' he protested. 'Remember last time? He was just going to put us on the beach so we could grab Rose and head straight back to the cinema. But it didn't work out like that, did it?'

Rose was Kip's six-year-old sister. She had

accidentally ended up on Terror Island, and Kip and Beth had been obliged to go in to the film to rescue her. Kip still had nightmares about his sister stuck on a sinking ship or being pursued by flesh-eating cavemen. It had been touch and go right up till the end of the film, and they'd only made their escape seconds before the closing credits rolled.

'I'll admit it wasn't plain sailing,' said Beth. 'But we'd be better this time. We've learned from the mistakes we made . . .'

'No way,' said Kip bluntly. He walked past her up the steps to the entrance. 'We should get moving,' he told her. 'The kids will be arriving in fifteen minutes and they'll be wanting their popcorn.'

Beth trudged after him. 'You know as well as I do you loved being in that film. You've been thinking of nothing else since we got back,' she insisted. 'Don't tell me you haven't. I've seen it on your face.'

'I'm not talking about this now,' whispered Kip, his hand on the door. 'Dad will hear us.'

'All right then, when *will* we talk about it?' asked Beth.

'Later.' He opened the door and stepped into the cinema.

CHAPTER TWO

Coke and Popcorn

Dad was sitting in the little office doing his paper-work and looking a lot happier than he had in a long while. He glanced up as Kip and Beth appeared in the doorway and gave them a grin.

'You two are cutting it a bit fine,' he said, glancing at his watch. He studied Beth for a moment. 'How's things?' he asked.

'OK.'

She sounded matter-of-fact, but Kip could tell she was still annoyed about his reluctance to go into *Spy Another Day*. That was the problem with Beth. She sulked about things.

Dad selected a sheet of paper from the desk and showed it to Kip. 'Got a quote in for the steam cleaning,' he said, and indicated a sum of money at the foot of the page.

Kip let out a long whistle. 'Jeez! I didn't realise you were going to buy an entire new cinema.'

'I'm not,' Dad assured him. 'Believe it or not,

that's what it costs. You've got to remember, Kip, this place hasn't had a proper clean since...'

'Nineteen twenty-three?' ventured Kip, referring to the year the cinema had opened for business.

'Well, probably more like the nineteen seventies,' said Dad. 'Minnie runs the hoover around once a week but that's just scraping the surface. There's more than thirty years of grime in here that needs shifting, so of course it's going to cost and arm and a leg. We'll need to get the seats re-upholstered too. It'll be worth it, though. Imagine coming in here and settling into a seat that feels as good as new.' He sighed and slipped the quote back into place. 'We might just have to wait another month or two, that's all. If business continues like it has been we'll be able to afford it for Christmas.' He glanced at his watch again. 'It's ten to two,' he said. 'Time to—'

'Get the popcorn on,' said Kip. He went into the adjoining confectionery booth and switched on the popcorn machine. Then he opened a huge bag of corn kernels and upended it into the mouth of the machine. The Paramount was showing the latest Pixar animation today and there was sure to be a big crowd. Before Mr Lazarus came on the scene

Kip had often presided over matinees that boasted no more than fifteen kids and their parents, little more than break-even point for the cinema. But when the mysterious old man had taken the post as the Paramount's projectionist he had brought with him the Lazarus Enigma – a machine of his own invention that made the films look and feel more 'real'.

The audiences who watched the films here had no way of knowing just how real they could be... How the Enigma could be used to actually send people into the films themselves. Only Kip and Beth had enjoyed that privilege – and Rose too, though after a little hypnosis from Mr Lazarus, she remembered very little about the experience.

Beth ambled into the booth and stood for a moment, looking glumly into the drinks chiller. 'We need more Cokes in here,' she muttered.

'No worries.' Kip squatted and reached under the counter for a new tray of drinks. When he stood up again, the tray of Cokes in his arms, he nearly let out a yell. A dark figure was at the counter gazing in at him – a tall, thin man with a full-length leather coat, a wide-brimmed fedora hat and the palest grey eyes in history.

'Mr Lazarus!' gasped Kip. 'What have I told you about creeping around like that?'

The old man's thin mouth curved upwards at the edges, but nobody would ever have described it as a smile. 'A thousand apologies, Kip,' he murmured in the lilting Italian-accented voice that Kip knew belonged to a man who was actually over 120 years old. 'I didn't mean to scare you.'

'I wasn't *scared*,' Kip assured him. 'Just a bit... spooked.'

Beth gave him a withering look. 'Are you sure?' she asked. 'Only you've gone really pale.'

'Don't be daft.' Kip set down the Cokes on the counter and started ripping at the plastic covering. Then he began to hand the cans to Beth, two at a time, so she could place them into the empty slots at the back of the chiller.

'And how is Beth?' inquired Mr Lazarus as though he were talking about somebody who wasn't actually there.

'Bored,' Beth answered, not even bothering to look at him. 'Bored and fed up.'

'Oh dear. I hate boredom. It's one of the worst crimes known to humanity. We'll have to see what we can do to liven things up for you.'

11

Kip glared at the old man. 'What's that supposed to mean?' he asked.

'Nothing. But if you two could pop up to the projection room once we've started running the film – there's something I'd like to discuss with you. A little...project I'm planning.' Mr Lazarus began to turn away but then seemed to think of something else. 'Oh, and, Beth, if you were to open the can of Coke you are presently holding in your right hand I think you may find something of interest. Kip, you should open the can in her *left* hand.' He reached into his pocket and put a couple of coins on the counter. 'My treat.'

And with that he turned away and went through the swing doors into the auditorium, moving as silently as a ghost.

Beth hesitated. She turned back and handed one can to Kip, then stared at the other.

She gave him an enquiring look but he could only shrug his shoulders. 'What's so interesting about a can of Coke?' muttered Beth.

'Search me,' Kip said.

She reached out her other hand, hooked her finger through the ring pull and yanked it open. There was a brief hiss, and a piece of tightly rolled paper slid smoothly up from the opening. Kip couldn't help noticing that it wasn't even wet.

He repeated the exercise with his can and a similar roll of paper appeared.

Beth set her drink down on the counter, pulled out the piece of paper and unrolled it. She held it out so that Kip could read it too.

CONGRATULATIONS!

You have been accepted as an agent of MI6.

Your code name will be 001.

Kip sighed, shook his head. He unrolled his own sheet of paper, which had exactly the same wording – except *his* code name was 002.

'How does he *do* that?' asked Beth.

'I don't know,' muttered Kip. 'I just wish he wouldn't.'

'And what does it mean?'

'What does *what* mean?' came Dad's voice from the office.

'Oh, er...nothing.' Kip crammed the slip of paper into the pocket of his jeans and motioned for Beth to do likewise. Then he lifted the open can to take a sniff of its contents and was amazed to find that it was still full of what appeared to be perfectly drinkable Coke.

Beth moved closer to whisper in Kip's ear. 'It's like he's a mind-reader or something.'

Kip frowned. He didn't have the first idea what Mr Lazarus was, but he was pretty sure that he was more accomplished than any television conjuror; he also had a shrewd idea what the old man was after.

'Better get a move on with that popcorn,' Dad reminded him. 'I reckon they'll be coming in any minute n—'

As if to prove his point the swing doors of the entrance burst open and a crowd of hyperactive kids ran yelling into the foyer followed by the poor, hapless adults who had been assigned to look after them for the afternoon. And also at that moment, as if on cue, with a loud popping sound and an absolutely mouthwatering smell, golden puffs of corn began to spill from the mouth of the machine into the heated glass cabinet.

'Show time,' said Kip and took up his position at the counter.

CHAPTER THREE

Mission Incredible

Once the film was in full swing and all latecomers had arrived, Kip and Beth made their excuses to his dad and went into the auditorium and up the stairs to the projection room.

The Paramount was packed this afternoon and, as he walked up the steps between the rows of seats, Kip was aware of how the young audience seemed absolutely spellbound by the film – there was none of the restlessness you would normally expect from kids at a movie show. The Lazarus Enigma was at work, keeping every set of eyes glued to the screen.

Kip pushed open the door of the projection room and stepped inside. Beth followed.

In the months since his arrival Mr Lazarus had added a lot of home comforts to the small, cluttered space. As well as the folding bed, where he liked to take the occasional nap, it also boasted a weird assortment of bits and pieces – strange items of antique furniture, stuffed animals, pieces of outmoded movie equipment. Maps and old posters were Blu-Tacked to the bare plaster walls, and over in one corner stood Mr Lazarus's latest acquisition – a big stainless-steel Gaggia coffee machine that looked like it belonged on the deck of the Starship Enterprise. Mr Lazarus loved coffee, but it couldn't be just a cup of instant, oh, no! He bought fresh coffee beans every week, ground them by hand and made cups of steaming espresso and Americano. Consequently the projection room was always filled with a mouthwatering aroma.

Of course, Kip knew the truth – that Mr Lazarus actually *lived* up here – but as far as Dad was concerned his projectionist rented a small flat just up the road, and merely liked to be surrounded by a few 'creature comforts' when he was at work. It was surely only a matter of time before Dad discovered what was really going on, but, for now, he was too absorbed by the Paramount's new-found success to take much notice of anything else.

Mr Lazarus was standing by the projector staring through the viewing window at the moving images dancing on the screen in the auditorium. For an instant the vividly coloured animations were reflected in his eyes, giving him a decidedly eerie look, but he glanced up when Kip and Beth came in and gave them a welcoming smile.

'Ah, here are my two assistants!' he exclaimed. He turned away from the projector and came towards them, grinning cheesily. 'Now, I'm sure you two would like a nice latte.' He didn't wait for an answer but went straight to the coffee machine and began making the drinks with well-practised ease. 'Beth, no sugar for you because you are sweet enough. Kip, I believe you take two big spoonfuls.' He shook his head in mock disapproval. 'As for me, I drink my coffee as it is meant to be drunk – strong and black.' He waved them over to a small round table and some vacant chairs. 'Please, sit,' he said. 'Make yourselves comfortable. This will only take a moment.'

'What's this all about?' asked Kip irritably. 'Only, I really should be helping Dad downstairs.'

'Nonsense! Nobody ever comes more than ten minutes after the film has started.' He held a jug of milk under a metal spout and hot steam hissed into it, making it froth. 'Who would do such a thing? Missing the start of a film is a crime. In my opinion, it should be punishable by imprisonment, the same for those idiots who insist on sitting in the row behind you unwrapping boiled sweets very slowly.' He spooned sugar into Kip's cup and then gave him a sly look. 'I have hardly seen you two for a while. It's starting to feel like you are . . . avoiding me.'

Kip sighed. 'It's just that Mum says homework is more important—'

'Than cinema? No offence to your mother, but that is nonsense. Nothing is more important! Why, every single thing I have learned in life I have learned from a cinema screen. And I am one of the cleverest people I know!'

'You said something about a project,' ventured Beth.

'Yes. Yes, I did.' Mr Lazarus came over to the table carrying a tray of coffee and a plateful of the little almond biscuits he always served. He set down the drinks and took a seat. 'You will be aware, I'm sure, that next week the Paramount is showing the new Jason Corder picture?'

'*Spy Another Day*!' cried Beth. 'Yes, I can't wait!'

Mr Lazarus indicated a couple of metal film canisters standing off in one corner. 'It may interest you to know that the film has already arrived. I asked the distributors to send it to me a few days early.'

Kip glared at Mr Lazarus suspiciously. 'Why would you do that?' he asked. 'You're not allowed to show it until the release date, which is next Friday.'

'I'm not allowed to show it to a paying audience – but that doesn't mean I can't arrange a private viewing for friends.' He waved a gloved hand at his companions then took a sip of his coffee and gave a sigh of pure pleasure. 'Actually, I was thinking of tomorrow morning, before the Sunday matinee. You'd be among the first people in the country to experience it.'

'Wow, brilliant!' cried Beth, but Kip still had his suspicions.

'There's more to it than that, isn't there?' he said.

There was a silence broken only by the clattering of the spools of film as they passed through the gate and the muffled sound of laughter coming from the auditorium below them.

'You have a suspicious nature, Kip,' Mr Lazarus told him eventually. 'But I'll admit there *could* be more to it. That rather depends on you two.' He leaned forward over the table as if to whisper a secret. 'One of my collector friends has asked me to get him something from the film . . . something that he is prepared to pay a great deal of money for.'

'I knew it,' said Kip bitterly. 'I knew there'd be a catch. Come on, Beth, we're not listening to any more of this . . .' He stood up from the table but his friend made no attempt to follow him.

'Let's hear him out first,' she said calmly.

'But, Beth, he wants us to . . .'

'It can't hurt to listen, can it?' Beth picked up her cup of coffee and took a sip. 'Go on,' she told the old man. 'Explain.'

Kip sank reluctantly back into his seat and Mr Lazarus smiled.

'My friend asked me if I could get Jason Corder's ID card, the one that has been featured in every film. You know it?'

'Yes,' said Beth. 'He always carries it in his left breast pocket. It has special software inside that means he can change the look of it to fit all his false identities. He has thirty-nine of them.'

'Excellent. I didn't know you were such a fan.'

'I've seen every film at least three times,' she said gravely.

'Bravo. Well, my friend is willing to pay whatever price I ask.'

'That's crazy,' muttered Kip. 'What's to stop you from getting a fake card printed up to sell to your friend.'

Mr Lazarus glared at him as though he had just used bad language. '*What's to stop me?* My honour, that's what! I wouldn't dream of trying to trick him. And do you honestly think a high-street printer could re-create something that can change its look to suit thirty-nine identities? No, it has to be the real thing, the kind of thing that only the Lazarus Enigma can bring into existence. So, I was thinking, if I could send you into one of the early scenes of the film . . .'

'No way!' Kip told him. 'We're not doing that again. We almost died last time. We nearly got eaten by Neanderthals.'

Mr Lazarus shrugged. 'Last time was different. Rose ended up in the film and you had to go straight in there to collect her. There was no time to prepare. This time you'll have the luxury of watching the scene through before you enter. You'll know exactly what's going to happen; you'll be able to just grab the ID card and leave. End of story.'

Kip was unconvinced. 'Something could still go

wrong,' he said. 'And, besides, why should I risk my neck?'

Mr Lazarus smiled. 'I've been thinking about your father's plans for the Paramount. You know, the steam-cleaning project?'

Kip scowled. 'What about it?' he asked.

'What if I were to pay for it . . . out of the money you helped me earn?'

'Dad would be really suspicious if you suddenly had loads of dosh.'

'He needn't know it came from me. I could be . . . an anonymous donor. Yes, I rather like the idea of that! I could just send in the cleaning company to do the work, paid in full. What a wonderful surprise for your father. And what a wonderful thing for the Paramount.'

'I don't know . . .' said Kip. 'I'd need to—'

'I'll do it,' said Beth.

Kip looked at her in amazement. 'What are you talking about?' he cried.

'You heard me.' Beth set down her coffee cup. 'I'll go into the film – since Kip is so scared of doing it.'

'I'm not scared!' protested Kip. 'I just think you shouldn't go rushing in there.'

'She won't,' Mr Lazarus assured him. 'As I said, she'll have time to prepare. Also, I've designed some rather nifty new equipment for her to take in with her. I—'

'Whoah! Hang on a minute!' This was all going too fast for Kip's liking. He turned to look at Beth. 'You know I can't let you go in there by yourself,' he said.

'Why not?'

'Because . . . well, because I . . . I can't let my . . . my best friend go in alone, can I?'

Beth gave him an odd look. 'Oh, so that's what we are then? Best friends? Not boyfriend and girlfriend?'

'Er . . . well, I . . .'

'That's what I *thought* we were. Only, I couldn't help but notice it hasn't been mentioned since we got back from the island. Like, three months ago?'

'Well, no, but . . . that's because I wasn't sure . . . I mean, I didn't know . . .' Kip was uncomfortably aware that Mr Lazarus was hearing every word of this. His voice trailed away and he took a despairing sip of his coffee. 'I was kind of waiting for you to say something.'

'Oh, were you? Well, it doesn't matter anyway.

24

I already said, I'd love to go in there and meet Daniel Crag, so—'

'But it wouldn't *be* Daniel Crag, would it? It would be Jason Corder...the super-spy. He wouldn't think twice about putting a bullet into somebody who got in his way.'

'He wouldn't shoot a woman,' Beth corrected him. 'That's never happened in any of the films. He's never even punched a woman. He *likes* women.'

'He likes them a bit too much, if you ask me! And, besides, what about the villains? They'd quite happily finish you off. They covered some poor woman in treacle in the last film and threw her onto an ant heap.'

'There won't *be* any villains in the scene Beth goes into,' Mr Lazarus assured him. 'I have already selected the scene. It'll just be her and Jason Corder, one-to-one.'

For some reason this bothered Kip even more than the thought of her running into the baddies.

'Well, obviously I'll have to come with you,' he told Beth. 'Somebody has to make sure you don't get into any trouble.'

'Don't put yourself out,' she snapped. 'I can look after myself.'

'No, you only *think* you can.'

'I saved your life.'

'What?'

'On Terror Island. I lopped that Neanderthal's head off. Not that I got any thanks for it.'

'Beth, that's not fair. I *did* thank you.'

'Yeah, like I'd passed you the salt or something.'

Kip shook his head in disbelief. He glared across the table at Mr Lazarus. Despite all his best intentions he had just ended up agreeing to something he knew was going to be dangerous.

'Just one thing,' he said. 'Remember, I said it was a bad idea from the beginning. So when it all goes horribly wrong—'

'You'll be able to say "I told you so"!' sneered Beth. 'Don't you know people hate it when you say that to them?'

There was another long silence before gales of laughter rose up from the auditorium. Kip didn't feel much like joining in.

'Nothing's going to go wrong,' Mr Lazarus assured them. 'Meet me here at ten o'clock tomorrow morning. That will give us plenty of time to study the sequence before you go in.'

'That's four hours before the matinee,' observed

Kip. 'Why would you need so long?'

Mr Lazarus's smile never faltered. 'We have to allow for the unforeseen,' he said. 'We have to be sure we have time to run the entire film, should we need to.'

'But if everything is as straightforward as you say, then—'

'Enough.' Mr Lazarus raised his cup of coffee. 'To our latest adventure!' he said. 'And to the continued success of the Paramount.' He drank, and Beth did likewise. But Kip sat there, staring into the pale brown depths of his latte, wondering just what exactly he had let himself in for.

CHAPTER FOUR

Interval

After the matinee Kip and his dad swept up the worst of the spilled popcorn and ice-cream wrappers then left Mr Lazarus to lock up. They got home around five and were greeted by the appetising smell of lasagna, their regular Saturday tea-time treat, cooking in the oven.

Dad went into the kitchen to help Mum, and Kip climbed the stairs to his room to check out Facebook on his computer. He knew he'd have to get stuck into his homework tonight in order to justify going to the cinema for ten o'clock tomorrow morning but he wasn't quite ready to make a start on it. He supposed he'd use the same excuse as before – that he'd be 'helping Mr Lazarus install some new equipment'. The last time he'd used it he'd been pretty much telling the truth. The 'equipment' had been the Lazarus Enigma.

There wasn't much happening on Facebook. Most of his friends were going on about what a boring weekend they were having and how they couldn't wait for the Christmas holidays. Kip imagined himself posting that he'd be taking a trip into a Jason Corder movie tomorrow and that there was every chance he'd wind up dead or tortured. But then he imagined how his friends would react and decided against it. Instead he simply said that he was *Looking forward to the new Triple Zero movie*, and left it at that.

There was a knock on his bedroom door and looking up he saw Rose standing in the doorway, gazing mournfully in at him. She was carrying her Barbie and Ken dolls, and she looked bored.

'Can I come in?'

'No, get lost,' he said grumpily, but she ignored him and came in anyway. Rose sat on his bed and stared at him blankly.

'What you doing?' she asked him.

'I'm knitting with marmalade,' he told her.

She made the face she always made when he said something silly, the look that said she was way more mature than he was and wasn't going to stoop to his level.

'You're on *Facebook*.' She managed to make it sound like an accusation. 'I want to be on Facebook but Mummy says no. She says you need to be thirteen.'

'You also need to have some friends,' Kip told her.

'I've got friends,' said Rose defensively. 'Only none of them are allowed on Facebook, either. Can I be on *your* Facebook?'

'It doesn't work like that,' he said. 'You'll just have to wait until you're thirteen.'

'That's *ages*,' she grumbled. 'Couldn't I pretend to be you and say stuff to all your friends?'

'No way! Look, haven't you got something you should be getting on with?'

She shook her head. 'I'm bored.'

Kip sighed. Another one. He wondered if all girls spent their time being bored.

'Will you play with me?' she pleaded. Rose held up the dolls just in case he hadn't noticed them. 'You can be Ken and I'll be Barbie and we could go on holiday together.'

'Aww... not now, Rose.' He felt guilty saying it, remembering how, just before he left Terror Island, he'd promised his sister he would be nicer to her, that he'd play with her and wouldn't ever complain again. That had lasted about a week before he'd finally snapped. 'I've... I've got stuff to do.'

'What stuff? You're only on the rotten old computer.' Her face suddenly rearranged itself into a very serious expression. 'I had that nasty dream again last night.'

'Did you?' Kip found he couldn't look her in the eye. This had come up a few times since their trip to Terror Island. 'The . . . same one?'

'Yes. I'm in that horrible building and I'm being chased by the Number Tails . . .'

'Neanderthals,' Kip corrected her.

'And they want to eat me. They chase me up onto this roof . . .'

'Yeah, I explained it before. It was the trailer you watched that time, you know, for *Night on Terror Island*?'

'There's a woman there with blonde hair, who I've seen in films. And you're there with Beth . . .' Rose lowered her eyelids for a moment. 'Your *girlfriend* . . .'

'She's not my girlfriend,' said Kip automatically.

'. . . And then there's this sound and this great big . . .' She paused as if trying to think of the word.

'Helicopter,' said Kip.

'Yes, it comes out of nowhere and somebody throws down a rope.' She paused again and gave him a suspicious look. 'How did you know I was going to say helicopter?'

'Er... because you... you must have told me before.'

'I don't think so.' She shook her head. 'There's never been a helicopter before. This was the first time.'

'Then I must have guessed. It's just a dream, Rose. It's nothing to worry about.'

'I know that. But why do I keep having it over and over?'

Mr Lazarus had warned Kip about this. He had made Rose 'forget' what had happened on the island but some small part of her, deep down inside, must have remembered bits of it and, from time to time, they came back to haunt her.

'I just wish it would stop,' she said dismally. 'It's scary.'

'You can say that again,' murmured Kip. He gave her what he hoped was a reassuring smile. 'But dreams can't hurt you, can they?'

His sister didn't answer that, just looked at him in silent accusation, prompting him to try and humour her. He pointed to the dolls. 'OK,' he said. 'Maybe just ten minutes.'

Rose got up off the bed, came over to him and thrust Ken into his hands.

'So . . . where are we going on holiday?' he asked her.

'Norwich,' she said, without hesitation. 'It's very nice at this time of year.' She pointed to the carpet. 'It's here,' she added. They settled themselves on the floor.

'Very exotic,' muttered Kip. 'What's in Norwich?'

'A caravan. One of those that doesn't have wheels, you know, like we saw in Rhyl that time? It's next to a crazy-golf course.'

'Sounds . . . great,' said Kip.

'Only we have to be careful cos of the baby.'

'What baby?'

'The one that Ken's going to have.'

'Don't you mean Barbie?'

'They're *both* going to have it, silly. And it's going to be called Madagascar.'

'Is that a boy or a girl?'

'Yes, it's one of those. I'm not sure which.'

Rose's world was a confusing place but Kip did his level best to stay with it. Ken and Barbie played a couple of rounds of imaginary crazy golf. Rose – or rather, Barbie – insisted on winning both games.

Whenever Kip/Ken took a shot Rose shook her head and told him he'd missed by miles.

Mum's voice drifted up the stairs, telling them that dinner was ready, and Kip tried not to look too relieved. He handed Ken back to Rose and got up off the carpet. 'Well, that was fun,' he said. 'We'll have to do it again some time.'

'After dinner?' suggested Rose.

'Can't,' he told her. 'Too much homework.'

She looked disappointed. 'Why do you always have so much homework?' she asked him.

It was a good question and one that Kip didn't really have an answer for. They went out of the bedroom and started down the stairs.

'Tomorrow morning, then.'

'Umm...can't do that, either. I have to help Mr Lazarus at the cinema.'

Rose made a face as though she'd just noticed an unpleasant smell.

'What?' asked Kip defensively.

'He's *weird*,' Rose said.

'No he's not. He's just old.'

'Old and weird,' insisted Rose. 'Don't you think there's something *funny* about him?'

'Like what?'

Rose shrugged. 'He talks funny.'

'That's just his Italian accent.'

'And he's always looking at you, like he knows something you don't. And why is he always at the cinema? He never seems to go *anywhere* else...'

'Shush,' said Kip nervously. They had reached the bottom of the stairs and were nearly within listening distance of the kitchen. 'Don't let Mum and Dad hear you,' he hissed.

'Why not?' asked Rose suspiciously.

'Because...they might...Look, just pipe down, OK? The Paramount is doing really well now and that's mostly because of Mr Lazarus. You don't want to spoil that, do you?'

'Well, no...'

Kip made a valiant attempt to change the subject. 'Hey, you're coming to the matinee tomorrow, aren't you?'

'Yes...'

'So, if you like, you can help me out in the confectionery stall until the film starts.'

Rose looked unimpressed. 'And I would do that because...?'

'Because if you do, I'll buy you an ice cream.'

She thought about it for a moment. 'OK,' she

said; happily, she seemed to have forgotten all about Mr Lazarus.

Kip allowed himself a smile and then he and Rose went into the kitchen for their dinner.

CHAPTER FIVE

Going In

Next morning Kip let himself quietly out of the house and trudged down the main street into the village. He had no reason to suppose that the trip into *Spy Another Day* would go well, if his two other movie visits were anything to go by. He'd dipped his toe in the water with *Public Enemy Number One*, going in for no more than ten minutes and, for his troubles, had nearly been knocked down by a runaway truck. He couldn't begin to list all the disasters that had occurred on Terror Island, and he could hardly believe that Beth had somehow managed to forget them. But he was committed to doing it now, so he supposed he'd just have to make the best of it – and, besides, he had to admit that, despite everything that had happened to him, there was still a part of him that was incredibly excited about the idea.

When he got to the cinema he found Beth sitting on the steps, waiting for him. They'd parted on bad terms yesterday, so he was a little wary of her. She was filling in the squares on one of her word-puzzle books, something she loved to do. She was particularly good at anagrams, but Kip could never get the hang of how to do them. He couldn't help noticing that she'd dolled herself up. She was wearing a black dress and sparkly tights and, when he got closer, he noticed she was even wearing some lip gloss and eye make-up.

'What's with the fancy-dress?' he asked her sullenly, and Beth gave him a glare, which made him realise that he hadn't sounded very complimentary. 'Er... I mean, you look... nice and everything, but...'

'Just wanted to look my best for Daniel,' she told him.

It was ridiculous but Kip couldn't help feeling a surge of jealousy. 'That's stupid,' he said. 'He's way too old for you. He must be like... forty, or something.'

Beth shrugged. 'That doesn't mean I can't look nice, does it?'

'I suppose not.' Kip climbed the steps to the entrance, unlocked the glass door and held it open for Beth. Then he glanced furtively along the street

38

before stepping inside and locking the door behind him.

They went straight into the auditorium and up the steps to the projection room, where they found Mr Lazarus waiting for them with two steaming lattes and a plate of biscuits.

'Right on time,' he said. 'I knew I could depend on you two. Now, if you'd like to grab your coffees and take your places at the viewing window, we'll study the scene I've selected for your visit.'

It seemed easy enough. The piece of film that Mr Lazarus had chosen was, he told them, one of the few scenes where Corder was alone. Following on from the explosive pre-credits sequence, it showed the spy walking along a narrow corridor and descending a metal staircase, on his way to a briefing session with his regular contact 'Z'.

As Mr Lazarus played it back and forth a few times, he outlined the plan. 'You'll appear in the corridor right in front of him. He'll be startled! One of you will distract him ... Beth, I suggest that is you, and, Kip, you will reach quickly into his inside breast pocket and grab the ID card. Then you'll take hold of Beth's hand and press the eject button on the Retriever.' He took the now-familiar chunk of Perspex from his pocket and hung it around Kip's neck on its length of chain. Beneath the protective metal cover, the eject button glowed with a pulsing red light. Mr Lazarus spread his hands in an 'easy-peasy' gesture. 'Simple,' he said. 'You'll be out of there before he has time to think.'

'I don't know...' Kip shook his head. 'Don't forget, Jason Corder is an expert in ty-phoo...'

'*Kai* Fu,' Beth corrected him. She looked at Mr Lazarus. 'It's an ancient Japanese art of self-defence. There are only three people in the world who are black belts and Jason is one of them. In *Diamonds Are Expensive* he took on fifteen armed assassins and beat them all without breaking sweat.'

Mr Lazarus waved a hand at her. 'That's very interesting, but it won't come to that. Even *his* reflexes can't deal with people who appear out of thin air.' He turned away, dismissing the idea. 'Now, come and look at the new equipment I've designed for you.' The projectionist hurried over to the worktop where he kept the Gaggia and picked up two tiny oval-shaped gadgets. He placed one into each of their hands. 'I give you the Communicator mark two!' he announced proudly.

Kip examined his item in more detail. Then he lifted it to his nose and sniffed at it. 'This is a coffee bean,' he said.

'What? Oh, sorry, they're about the same size . . .' Mr Lazarus took back the beans and had another look on the cluttered worktop. 'Er . . . wait, I . . . Ah, yes!' This time the two little ovals he picked up were silver. 'I had a look at the original system,' he explained. 'All that Bakelite. So nineteen-fifties, don't you think? So I went back to the drawing board. These are state of the art. In fact, if the people at Apple ever find out about them they'll be coming after me waving their cheque books.' He took two more devices from the worktop and pushed one into each of his ears, then gestured for Kip and Beth to insert theirs. They did as he suggested.

'Now, what do you think of that?' he asked them.

Kip had to suppress a gasp – Mr Lazarus's voice was deep in his ear, a tiny compressed sound that was as clear as crystal. Then Mr Lazarus took another gadget from his pocket and spoke again. Now the voice was gone from Kip's ear but Beth gave a thumbs up. Kip was impressed. 'How do we turn them on and off?' he asked.

'You don't. I will hear your voices, one in each ear, whatever you say.' He showed Kip the gadget in his hand. 'This little rocker switch allows me to move between the two of you,' he explained. 'Otherwise it could get confusing.' He pushed the switch one way. 'Testing, testing,' he said and the voice was back in Kip's ear. Then the old man rocked the switch the other way and repeated the phrase, and once again, Beth reacted with a thumbs up.

'What if you need to hear both of us at the same time?' asked Kip.

Mr Lazarus gave him a rather cross look. 'I can't do that,' he said. 'And, besides, that would be very confusing. Imagine the two of you trying to shout over each other. No, I can just keep rocking the switch back and forth, it's easy enough.'

Kip stared at him intently. 'You're sure you've thought everything through?' he asked. 'Only, we don't want anything to go wrong, do we?'

'What could possibly go wrong?' roared Mr Lazarus. He clapped his gloved hands together and let out a hearty laugh, but Kip didn't feel like joining in. The old man was undoubtedly a brilliant inventor but he was over one hundred years old and tended to forget things. Kip and Beth could very easily have gone into the film with coffee beans in their ears!

'Now, I think we're about ready to send you into your mission,' Mr Lazarus announced. He walked across to the projector and reversed the film to the start. Then he pulled the black sheet off the Lazarus Enigma.

It looked so innocent: just a short length of well-oiled metal track, on which stood a round wooden platform that could be pushed backwards and forward into a powerful beam of light that was reflected down from a large glass prism. But Kip knew only too well what it was capable of.

Mr Lazarus pointed to the platform. 'If you would like to take your positions.'

Kip and Beth exchanged glances. Now it had come to it Beth didn't seem half as confident as before. She was regarding the platform nervously and, in the gloom of the projection room, her face seemed unnaturally pale.

'We don't have to go through with this,' said Kip quietly.

She glanced at him. 'Sure we do.'

'No, really, we don't. Nobody will blame you if you back down... Will they, Mr Lazarus?' He looked at the old man but he didn't say anything, just stood there with that weird smile on his face. It suddenly seemed very quiet in the room. Then Beth took a deep breath and, walking forward, she stepped onto the platform and stood there waiting. Kip scowled, but went to join her. He climbed on so he was face to face with her.

'Now, hold on really tightly to each other,' Mr Lazarus warned them.

Kip took hold of Beth's hands, noting as he did so that his were slippery with sweat. He was also experiencing a sinking feeling in the pit of his stomach.

'You sure you've got the film lined up properly?' His voice was little more than a strangled croak.

'Yes, yes, don't worry about a thing. I'm going to start a few moments before your scene and then I'll count you down from three and slide you in just at the right moment.' Mr Lazarus was turned away, busying himself with the projector, but his voice was ringing in Kip's right ear. 'OK, I'm switching on now.' The projector light brightened and the reels began to turn, casting a flickering beam of light through the hatch. From the auditorium came the muffled sounds of warfare – guns hammering, bombs exploding, people yelling at each other.

'What's that?' whispered Beth.

'Relax, it's just the end of the pre-credits sequence,' said Mr Lazarus. 'Far too dangerous to send you in there, of course, what with the weapons and everything. Ah, now here come the opening credits.'

Music swelled and a woman's voice began to warble the corny theme song.

'Spy another day
Live to cry another day
When a lover begs you stay
That's the time to leave . . .
To spy another day
Learn to try another day
When there's a hand of cards to play
To win you must believe . . .'

'What a rubbish song,' muttered Kip.

'I quite like it,' said Beth. 'At least it's better than the last one. But then, what could anyone do with a title like *Diamonds Are Expensive?*'

'Look,' said Kip. 'I need to say something to you before we leave. When we're in there . . .'

'Yes?'

'Try and stay out of trouble. I mean, don't go looking for it, you know what I'm saying?'

She stared back at him. 'No, not really.'

Kip sighed. There was a long, rather tense silence, during which the music swelled for the chorus – violins soaring behind the vocalist's awful lyrics.

'Don't ask why another day,
Reach the sky another day
Learn to fly another day . . .'

Kip tried to find the right way to tell her what he wanted to say. 'Well, it's just that you can be a bit reckless.'

'Me? Who says?'

'I do. I mean, you're the one who volunteered us for this . . . and last time, on the island and everything . . . well, you did a few daft things, didn't you?'

'What, you mean like saving your life?'

'No, that was one of the better things.'

'Oh, thanks.'

'But what I'm saying is, you know, if things get hairy in there . . . and they probably will, it's best if you leave everything to me.'

'What, you're a hairdresser now?'

'You know what I mean! I'm just saying . . .'

'Get ready!' warned Mr Lazarus. 'The song is about to finish...'

'...It's going to be dangerous in there and...'

'Three...two...one...GO!'

The last word cracked so loudly in Kip's ear, he lifted his right hand to touch it. In the same instant Mr Lazarus gave the oiled wooden platform a push with his foot, launching it forward into the light reflecting down from the projector. Caught off balance, Kip and Beth struggled to stay upright, the blinding white light blazed in their eyes and the familiar melting sensation overcame them. Then they were whirling downwards into the light, spinning dizzily around, and Kip was aware of his sweaty left hand desperately trying to retain its grip on Beth's right hand – trying and failing. His last impression was of her fingers sliding through his grasp and then she was gone.

Kip opened his mouth to yell Beth's name but suddenly, shockingly, he was in the film, flying feet first through the air. His boots slammed hard between the shoulder blades of a man a few steps ahead of him, a man in a stylish grey suit who went lurching forward towards the top of a metal staircase, grabbing frantically for the handrail and missing.

Gravity took over. Kip dropped through the air. His backside connected with a steel platform, sending a searing jolt of pain through his buttocks and he just about registered that the man he had slammed into was now tumbling head over heels down the stairs, out of sight. Kip lay for a moment, stunned. He groaned and struggled upright, rubbing his bottom with his hands. He moved slowly to the top of the stairs and looked down them. The man lay on his back on the floor below, his eyes shut. It was Jason Corder.

'Oh, no!' said Kip.

'*Kip?*' The familiar voice in his ear nearly made him jump out of his skin.

'Oh! Er . . . Mr Lazarus. I've just . . . I think I've just knocked Jason Corder down some stairs.'

'I know you have! I'm watching you on the screen right now. Why did you want to go and do a thing like that?'

'It was an accident! He was just . . . there.'

'Hmm. He's not . . . dead, is he?'

'Not sure. I hope not.' Kip went apprehensively down the steps. He kneeled beside Corder and shook his shoulder. The man was clearly out cold but his chest was rising and falling. 'No, I think it's OK; he's still breathing.'

'Well, that's a relief!' There was a pause. 'Right, Kip, this isn't how we planned it but it's a golden opportunity. Just reach into his inside pocket and get his ID.'

Kip frowned but did as he was told. The card was right where it was supposed to be. He pulled it out and had a quick glance at it. The photo currently showed Corder's face, but Kip knew that with a little computer jiggery-pokery it could be made to look like any one of thirty-eight other people, with false details to match. He slid the card into his back pocket.

'Got it,' he announced.

'Piece of cake,' said Mr Lazarus. 'Now you can press the eject button and come back.'

That was when it hit Kip. He stood up and looked slowly around the spacious hallway. There was not another living soul in sight.

'Where's Beth?' he asked quietly.

CHAPTER SIX

Bungle in the Jungle

At first Beth was spinning round and round in the midst of a blinding white light – then suddenly, unexpectedly, she was crashing downwards through thick vegetation, leaves and branches lashing at her arms and legs as she flailed through them. She just had time to register that she didn't seem to be where she was supposed to be when the ground came racing to meet her and she thudded face-up into a tangle of thick ferns and bushes. The springy undergrowth helped break her fall a little but the impact was still enough to drive the breath out of her lungs. She rolled onto her side and lay there for a moment, gasping, trying to gather her scrambled thoughts.

She was suddenly aware of the smells of exotic flowers all around her, the chirruping of insects and a dank, oppressive heat that seemed to sap the energy from her limbs. For a terrible moment she thought she was back on Terror Island and fear coiled like a snake in her belly. Then a huge multicoloured butterfly the size of a large bat flapped past her and Beth sat up, gazing around.

Maybe not the island, she thought, but she *was* in a jungle and, after her last experience somewhere like this, it was really not the kind of place she wanted to be. Wasn't she supposed to be on a metal platform, ready to meet Daniel Crag? Something had clearly gone badly wrong. Beth got unsteadily to her feet, shaking her head to dispel the muzzy feeling that lingered there. Then she turned slowly in a circle, hoping to see Kip . . . But the jungle lay all around her. It seemed to stretch for miles in every direction and there was no sign of human life.

'Where am I?' she muttered. She remembered that she was still wearing her earpiece and desperately tried to make contact. 'Uh, Mr Lazarus? Are you there?' No answer. Either the device had failed or he was switched to Kip's channel. She kept talking anyway, hoping that he'd hear something. 'Umm . . . I'm in the middle of a jungle. There's . . . Ooh!' She broke off and took a couple of steps backwards as a brightly coloured lizard skittered through the grass a metre in front of her. 'I'm confused,' she said. She turned in another circle.

'I'm not where you said I'd be. What should I do? There's no sign of Kip.'

Still no answer. Beth tried to think logically about her situation. Obviously she wasn't where she was supposed to be in the film, which meant that she had to be in another scene. But which one? And how far into the film was it? She knew only too well what it meant if she was still there when the closing credits rolled, though Mr Lazarus had never mentioned anything like this.

'I've got to get out of here,' she said, trying to fight the rising sense of panic she felt. 'But I don't know what to do. I can't just stand here twiddling my thumbs. Mr Lazarus, ARE YOU THERE?'

Silence, save for the chirruping of insects and the stirring of foliage.

Beth gazed hopelessly this way and that through the green depths that surrounded her, until she finally spotted what looked like a narrow trail leading off through the undergrowth. With no better option she started along it, ducking her head to scoot under low-hanging bushes and ferns. The awful heat wrenched big beads of sweat from all over her body and, after walking just a short distance, her best dress was sodden. It occurred to her that although she had worn it to impress Daniel Crag, after being quite literally dragged through a hedge backwards, she must look an absolute fright, and she was quite grateful that he couldn't see her right now. Her bare arms were scratched and scraped from her fall through the foliage, and her tights were laddered and torn in several places. As if to make things even worse, an irritating halo of flies appeared from out of the bushes and started buzzing inquisitively around her head. She was obliged to tear off a palm frond so she could swat them away as she walked.

After what seemed like an hour's aimless trudging through the green depths, Beth emerged from the thick undergrowth onto a scrub-covered hillside. It dropped steeply away into a lush valley where a winding river shimmered in the sunlight. Halfway down the hill, sticking up about half a metre from the ground, was a square stone hatch. It looked out of place there, the only man-made object in a sea of vegetation, but the sight of it gave her hope that there must at least be some form of civilised life around here.

Beth began to descend the hill, placing her feet with care – she didn't want to miss her footing and take the quick route down.

When she reached the hatch she saw it was covered by a honeycomb of thick steel bars clamped in position by a heavy padlock. She kneeled beside the hatch and peered through the bars. She could see a series of metal rungs, set into a circular stone shaft below, leading straight down into the earth. At intervals, electric safety lights dimly illuminated the descent, but Beth couldn't see an end to them. It must be an awfully long way down.

She considered for a moment and decided that, whatever was down there, it had to be a better option than wandering aimlessly through a jungle – so, after a few moments of deliberation, she searched around until her gaze finally fell on a rock the size of a coconut. Beth picked it up and carried it over to the hatch. Then she lifted it above her head and pounded it down onto the padlock, once, twice, three times, the impact shuddering along the lengths of her arms, the effort making her grunt. The sound of the blows seemed to echo down into the ground far below her. On her seventh attempt the lock broke open and fell between the bars. Beth paused and began to count. She had reached number eleven before she heard the distant thud of the shattered lock connecting with the ground. She swallowed nervously, reminding herself that it wouldn't be a good idea to lose her footing in there. But there wasn't much choice in the matter, so she lifted the heavy bars and pushed them to one side. She stared into blackness for a moment and her stomach lurched but she forced herself to stay calm. 'You'll be fine,' she muttered. 'Just don't look down.'

Beth clambered up onto the edge of the hatch, turned herself round and lowered her left foot gingerly until it found the first rung. She wished she'd worn boots instead of the elegant heeled shoes she'd chosen, but there was nothing she could do about that now. She gripped the stone edge of the hatch, lowered her right foot to the next rung and then started to descend.

Kip looked desperately around the deserted stretch of hallway. There was no sign of Beth anywhere. He was beginning to get a very bad feeling about this.

'Where can she be?' he asked the voice in his head.

'I was going to ask you the same question. I assumed she was just out of camera shot. What have you done with her?'

'I haven't done anything.' Kip looked frantically around again, and then it all came back to him in a vivid flash of memory. 'I lost my grip on her,' he gasped. 'I remember now. It was when we were coming in. I felt her hand slide through mine.'

'You let go of her?'

'Not on purpose! My hands were sweaty and . . .'

'Oh, this is bad. Very bad.'

'What do you mean? Where is she, Mr Lazarus?'

'She must have spun off in another direction. That can happen if you don't hang onto people tightly enough. I did warn you.'

'I couldn't help it, my hands were all slippy!'

'Well, I suppose it can't be helped. She'll be somewhere else in the film. Yes, she has to be! She'll have skipped on a scene or two, like a pebble bouncing across the surface of the water.'

It went horribly quiet for a moment. 'Mr Lazarus, I—'

'Shush! I'm thinking. What to do, what to do? Well, obviously I should be able to talk to her through the Communicator. Yes, I'll try and establish exactly where Beth is. Then you'll simply have to find her.'

'What?' Kip stood there, his mind racing. 'How am I supposed to do that?'

'You'll make your way through the film until you meet up with her. Once I make contact, I'll be able to advise you of the best way to proceed.'

'That's crazy! There must be some other way.' Kip stood there, his mind racing. 'Can't I . . . can't I come out of the film now and then we'll watch it through, back at the cinema, and I'll just pop back in when we get to *her* bit?'

'I'm not supposed to interrupt the flow of the film,' Mr Lazarus told him. *'It's too risky.'*

'But . . . you did when we were on the island, you put the film in reverse and all sorts.'

'That was an emergency! I had no other choice. Don't you know it's dangerous to mess around like that? I didn't tell you at the time but that can have awful consequences for the people involved. Oh yes, they can go mad – they can sometimes disappear altogether. Why, in Venice, there was a boy who used to go into films for me . . . Paolo was his name. I remember one time he came out of a film in a sticky moment and then tried to go back in again and . . . Well, that was the last anyone ever saw of him. A terrible time I had trying to explain that one.'

'Oh, that's great news. You lost a boy? How come you never mentioned this before?'

'I didn't want to worry you.'

'Worry me? That's a good one. Coming into these movies isn't worrying, it's terrifying. What if I can't find Beth?'

'You'll have to. The thing is not to panic. Remember, everything is going to run in real time for you but I'll be watching the edited version. You could feel like you're in there for months but in the real world it will only take two hours.'

'What . . . what if I don't find her in time?'

'Failure is not an option. If it gets to the closing credits, you'll both be trapped in there for ever. So I'd get moving if I were you.'

'Oh . . . perfect.' Kip thought for a moment. 'You knew this could happen, didn't you? That's why you left enough time for the whole film to run.'

'We had to be prepared for any eventuality. But, listen, we're wasting time. First things first. You'd better hide Corder. If somebody finds him, they'll realise something's up and they might prevent you from looking for Beth.'

Kip shook his head in disbelief, but he grabbed the secret agent's feet, dragged him across the hallway and pushed him into a gloomy corner.

As Kip straightened up he heard footsteps on the metal walkway above him.

'There's somebody coming!' he hissed.

'Well, don't just stand there. Hide!'

Kip looked frantically around and saw that there was only one possibility – a plain metal doorway at the top of the hall. As quietly as he could, he ran towards it. Thankfully the door wasn't locked. He opened it, stepped quickly inside and closed it again, then he flinched at the sound of a rather posh voice behind him.

'Ah, Agent Triple Zero, there you are! You're a few minutes late . . . but I have to say, that's the most incredible disguise I've ever seen.'

CHAPTER SEVEN

Down the Hatch

It was cramped and airless in the vertical shaft, and after just a few minutes Beth was soaked in fresh sweat. It wasn't so bad when you were by one of the dull safety lights because at least you had a sense of where you were, but several of them had failed and she had to descend whole stretches in almost total darkness, probing with an outstretched foot to find the next rung down, gripping the ones above her with hands that were slippery with perspiration. When she looked up it was to see that the circular opening of the hatch above her had already shrunk to the size of a manhole cover, and still she seemed to be no nearer to reaching the safety of the ground below.

'*Beth, are you receiving me?*'

Mr Lazarus's voice in her ear startled her so much she nearly lost her grip on the rungs. 'Oh, *now* you get in touch!' she cried. 'Where've you been?'

'*I've been trying to help out Kip. He's in a bit of a fix. Can you tell me exactly where you are?*'

'I'm down a ruddy great hole.'

'There's no need to be sarcastic, my dear!'

'I'm not being sarcastic. Can't you see me?'

'No. At the moment I'm watching Kip, on screen, but that could change at any moment. How did you end up in a . . . "ruddy great hole"?'

'I landed in this jungle and I couldn't get in touch with you, and then I saw this kind of hatch thing sticking up out of the ground so I decided to climb down it . . .'

'What made you do a dangerous thing like that?'

'Believe it or not, it seemed like a good idea at the time.'

'Hmm. Well, you've obviously arrived in a different part of the film from Kip. He's where you were supposed to be, with Jason Corder.'

'Lucky him! I don't suppose he fancies swapping places with me?'

'He doesn't have any choice over that . . . look, I'll have to go. Kip has knocked out Jason Corder and I think he's just been mistaken for him.'

'Are you trying to be funny? Kip's nothing like Jason Corder!'

'Yes, I know, but this can happen with characters in films. I've seen it before. It's like they are running on

automatic pilot. The script has led them to expect somebody and, no matter who turns up instead, they continue to see that person as the one they were expecting. Am I making any sense to you?'

'Not really. Can't Kip just explain who he really is? That he's there by accident . . . ? Hello?'

No answer. Mr Lazarus must have switched channels again. Beth cursed and continued with her descent.

She passed into an area where there were no more working safety lights and she was plunged into total darkness. She kept going, feeling her way with her hands and feet, moving slowly and carefully, inching herself down . . . And then she became aware of a rustling noise somewhere below her, the sound of dry leaves blowing across concrete. She paused and tried to look over her shoulder but there was total darkness below and she had no idea how far it was to solid ground. Beth took a deep breath and lowered a foot to find the next rung – and suddenly, horribly, something was flapping frantically beneath her heel – then there was a restless stirring all around her as unseen shapes launched themselves into the air and began to beat their leathery wings about her head.

Bats! The thought struck her at the same instant as her heel slipped and she dropped to hang at arm's length from one of the rungs. Air stirred around her face and Beth tried to tell herself that the bats would not touch her, that in this darkness they could see more clearly than she. But even as she thought it one of the shapes alighted on her shoulder – she gave a grunt of revulsion as she felt its furry body brush against her cheek. Then her wet hands were losing their grip and she was falling, falling through darkness...

Beth opened her mouth to scream but, as she did so, her feet struck firm ground. Her knees buckled beneath her and she tipped sideways, striking her head against something hard. A million fireworks seemed to explode in her brain, and then total darkness replaced them, flooding through her senses like spilled ink...

Kip turned to see a familiar grey-haired man, a character he had seen in dozens of Jason Corder movies, always played by the same actor. He was dressed in a smart pinstripe suit, and he was sitting at a desk, smiling welcomingly. Kip had no option but to smile back and try to look as though he belonged there.

'Hello, Z,' Kip said, because that was what the man called himself. 'How...how are you?'

'I'm fine, Triple Zero, just fine. Who did the disguise?'

Kip stared at him open-mouthed. 'Er...it was... umm...'

'*Department seventeen*,' whispered a voice in his ear.

'Er...yes! It was department...umm...s-seventeen,' muttered Kip.

'Seventeen? Don't think I've heard of them.'

'They're...new,' said Kip. 'Brand new. Hardly anyone knows about them. Top secret.' He tapped the side of his nose, a gesture he'd seen Corder make in other films. 'Absolutely hush-hush,' he said.

'Oh, yes, of course. So how did they...?' Z gestured at Kip. 'I mean, I understand how they changed the looks, and even the voice...But you must be a foot shorter.'

'Umm...'

'*New techniques*,' murmured Mr Lazarus.

'New tech freaks,' said Kip, mishearing. 'This is the first time they've ever been used.' He attempted

64

a devil-may-care laugh, which didn't quite come off. 'Just so long as they manage to put me back together again, eh?'

'Yes indeed, Triple Zero, yes indeed! New tech freaks, eh? My, my. You learn something new every day in this job. Well, don't just stand there, old boy, let's get you briefed.' He pressed a button on his desk and a steel plate in the floor silently slid open. A leather chair rose up from below, its base filling the opening exactly. Z waved him to it. 'Take a seat and we'll go through protocol.'

Kip nodded and walked across to the chair, trying desperately to remember what 'protocol' involved. He hoped it wasn't going to be painful.

Z pushed another button and a panel on the far wall slid aside to reveal a huge plasma screen. Then he held out a hand as though he wanted something. Kip looked at him blankly.

'Well, come along, man, haven't you got something for me?'

'Umm . . . I'm not sure I . . .'

'*He wants the ID!*' prompted Mr Lazarus.

'Oh, right,' said Kip, and Z gave him an odd look.

'Come along, Triple Zero! Goodness me, I think you're taking this new identity a little too seriously. You don't have to stay in character all the time.'

Kip reached into his back pocket and handed Z the card. He kept glancing nervously at the door, half expecting a furious Jason Corder to come crashing through it at any moment.

Z pushed the card into a slot in the desktop and instantly a complex sequence of flashing lights appeared on the screen, followed by the word AUTHENTICATED. The card slid out again and Z passed it back to Kip.

'I know it's ridiculous but we have to take precautions,' he explained. 'Why, for all I know, you could be a genuine schoolboy who's somehow managed to bluff his way in here!' There was a pause and then Z gave a strange guffawing laugh.

'*Join in with him*,' suggested Mr Lazarus.

Kip managed to force out a high-pitched cackle, but it couldn't have been very convincing because, after a few moments, Z stopped laughing, as though somebody had flicked a switch. His face became deadly serious. 'Watch the screen, Triple Zero,' he instructed. 'This transmission was sent to the United Nations less than an hour ago.'

He pressed a button but the screen remained

blank. The man leaned over the desk and pressed another couple of buttons. Still nothing happened. Z muttered something under his breath, then he lifted a hand and slammed down his fist hard on the desktop.

The screen shimmered and an image appeared. A figure was sitting in a high-backed leather chair in an empty room. The lighting was arranged in such an ingenious way that the person appeared only as a dark silhouette, but Kip could see that whoever it was wore black leather gloves and was stroking a white Burmese cat which lay on his lap. A deep, rumbling voice spoke:

'People of the world. I am Doctor Leo Kasabian. Hear my name and tremble!' There was a short silence as though the man was expecting some kind of reply to this. When there wasn't one, he continued, 'My demands are simple: one hundred billion dollars in cash, to be delivered by helicopter to a place of my choosing by midnight tomorrow. If the money is not received I shall activate... the Kasabian Annihilator.' There was another long pause. 'I expect you're wondering what that actually means. Well, allow me to explain...' A screen behind the doctor lit up and the camera moved closer. The setting appeared to be a laboratory. A line of six huge, grey creatures were standing in a row, all of them apparently identical. A couple of white-coated scientists stood either side of them, looking on proudly. The creatures were sort of human looking, but a foot or so taller than the scientists and obviously much, much heavier. They had ugly, slab-like faces covered in thick, leathery skin, and each of them had a curved horn sticking out of its forehead. They were dressed in armour – an ingenious metal helmet that fitted neatly around the horn, a breastplate, camouflage trousers and long leather boots. Each of them was cradling a vicious-looking assault rifle in its powerful arms. They were all staring straight at the camera, their tiny eyes glittering with brutish malice.

Kasabian's voice continued over the scene. 'Let me introduce you to an entirely new species … Rhino sapiens – half man, half rhinoceros! The most powerful fighting force on the planet, cloned by a team of top scientists in my secret laboratory and trained to carry out my bidding. Observe!' As if at some spoken command the rhino sapiens lifted their rifles and aimed them at the camera – then unleashed a deadly barrage of gunfire, apparently trying to kill the camera operator. The scientists covered their ears with their hands and moved out of harm's way as the screen filled with smoke.

The camera pulled back to reveal Kasabian's silhouette, hunched in his chair, still stroking the cat. 'Relax. They are firing blanks,' he said calmly. 'For the moment. What you have just seen are six prototypes, the first to emerge from the Kasabian Annihilator. But, when I fully activate the machine, it will begin to create an army of invincible warriors at the rate of five hundred troops every thirty minutes, one thousand troops an hour, twenty thousand troops a day...'

'Twenty-*four* thousand!' hissed a female voice just out of camera shot.

Kasabian paused for a moment. 'Er...yes... twenty-*four* thousand,' he corrected himself. 'Those troops will march straight out of the Annihilator to a fleet of helicopters, waiting to carry them to all the major capitals of the world. Their mission will be to take each capital by force and to enslave humanity. There will be bloodshed on an unprecedented scale, but my warriors will win because their armoured hide makes them virtually bulletproof. And I can simply create more troops to take the place of any that are killed. Once the world's forces have surrendered, I will appoint myself king, and anyone who opposes me will be ruthlessly eliminated.' He laughed, a deep, chilling sound that made the hairs on Kip's neck prickle.

'Yes, it would be an absolute nightmare – a nightmare from which the world would never recover. You probably doubt that I can do what I say, but believe me, I can. It would be as easy as that.' He tried to snap his fingers but no sound came out. 'If I could even be bothered to do it,' he added. 'You have twenty-four hours to comply with my demands. Well . . . when I say twenty-four, I mean' – the figure lifted a wrist to look at his watch – 'ooh, about twenty-three hours and fourteen minutes. Act quickly or pay the price.' The screen went blank. Then it came on again and Kasabian's deep voice continued. 'You're probably wondering where to deliver the money,' he said. 'Well, I'll tell you. The Sainsbury's car park, Weston-super-Mare. At midnight tomorrow. The helicopter must be fully fuelled. The pilot is to abandon it and walk away . . . On no account must he return to the helicopter. If anybody attempts to follow it, I will activate . . . The Kasabian Annihilator' – he lifted a gloved hand and wiggled an index finger – 'with this. And then you'll be really, really sorry.' There was a long pause before he muttered, 'You can stop filming now.'

The screen went black again. Z pressed a button and a cover slid halfway across the screen then appeared to jam. Z muttered something. He thumped the desktop again and the cover slid the rest of the way. He turned his attention back to Kip.

'We're taking no chances on this,' he said. 'We're talking to the appropriate people about obtaining the money but, in the meantime, we're sending you in, Triple Zero. We can't allow madmen to hold this planet to ransom. Obviously, with less than twenty-four hours to the deadline, there's no time to waste. So it's up to you to save the world.'

CHAPTER EIGHT

Mistaken Identity

Beth gradually came back to consciousness. She lay where she was for a moment as her senses returned. Then she sat up, rubbing her head with the flat of one hand, while she took stock of her situation.

She was sitting in near darkness on a dry, dusty, metal floor. Above her towered the upright shaft, down which she had recently fallen. When she looked up she could see a distant circle of blue sky – from here it appeared to be the size of a ten-pence piece. To the left and right of her stretched a seemingly endless oblong metal tunnel, most probably some kind of ventilation system, Beth decided. As if confirming her guess, a waft of stale-smelling warm air came billowing along the tunnel, stirring her hair. Deciding that she couldn't just stay where she was, she got herself onto her hands and knees and started crawling. It was cramped and warm in there, and after moving just a short distance her tights were gone at the knees and her best dress was soaked with sweat again, making her wish once more that she'd opted for scruffy jeans and a T-shirt.

'*Beth, how are things with you?*'

She was relieved to hear Mr Lazarus's voice, but, at the same time, rather irked that he sounded so calm and matter-of-fact.

'Not great,' she told him as she crawled along. 'There were bats, and I slipped and fell. I knocked myself out for a while. Now I seem to be in some kind of ventilation tunnel.'

'*I see. Listen, I can't stay on for long; Kip is in a bit of a pickle.*'

'Oh is he really? Meanwhile, don't worry about me, I'm having a great time.'

'*Er. . . I'll check back with you in a few moments.*'

'Thanks a bunch.'

She scrambled along for what seemed an age, then became aware of sounds from up ahead of her: the constant rattle and hum of machinery. Beth came to a metal grille set in the right-hand wall of the tunnel and paused to peek through it. She was looking into a vast underground chamber that appeared to have been carved out of volcanic rock. There were large pieces of machinery dotted around the place, great hulking metal constructions that winked and glittered with hundreds of dials and coloured lights. There were metal walkways connecting the constructions, overhead gantries with cranes that could move backwards and forward on oiled wheels; in and around all the hardware moved scores of men wearing white overalls and smoked-glass-fronted helmets that meant you couldn't see their faces. Some of them carried clipboards, while others just seemed to be milling aimlessly around, turning levers and checking dials, apparently at random. From hidden vents in the rock, clouds of steam rose and drifted towards the roof of the chamber.

Beth stared through the grille. She had seen enough Jason Corder films to know that this had to be the lair of the villain – they were the only people who had secret underground hideaways and employed dodgy-looking guys in white overalls. Furthermore, she knew that the Lazarus Enigma had the power to turn what must have in reality been no more than a collection of flashy-looking junk and film-set into something that could actually do what it was supposed to. If that machinery was supposed to be able to destroy the world then right now it would be quite capable of doing exactly that.

Beth felt a cold chill ripple through her.

'*Beth? Everything all right?*'

'Not really.'

'*Tell me exactly what's happening?*'

Beth described what she could see.

'*Hmm. It would seem you have ended up in the worst possible place in the film. I have just heard that the world is being held to ransom by a Doctor Leo Kasabian... Does this name mean anything to you?*'

'No. But they always have a new villain in each film.'

'*I see. Well, it seems likely that the place you're in is some kind of secret hideout. Now, I'm sorry, but I really need to get back to Kip.*'

'Yes, but just a minute,' hissed Beth. 'I...'

She broke off and edged away from the grille as a pair of white-suited men came to a halt just in front of it; but they were turned away from her so, after a few moments, she leaned closer again to listen into their conversation, which was slightly muffled beneath their helmets.

'Is everything done?' asked the first man.

'Yes, sir, all primed and ready to go. All it needs now is one word from Doctor Kasabian and Operation Snapple can be initiated.' The man's helmeted head shook from left to right. 'It'll be the end of the world as we know it.'

Beth frowned. She didn't much like the sound of this. She also didn't like the fact that something was tickling her ankle...

She glanced down and saw that a black, hairy spider the size of her fist was crawling up her leg.

'Make an excuse,' said the voice in Kip's ear. *'Tell him you can't go on a secret mission. Not right now. You need to look for Beth.'*

'Umm...right.' Kip gazed at Z across the desk. 'I'd...love to go, I really would,' he said. 'But...I have some homework to finish.'

Z rolled his eyes. 'Triple Zero, your attempts to remain in character are commendable, but I need you to pay attention.' He pressed a button and a drawer in the desk opened suddenly, thumping him in the stomach. He doubled over for a moment, his face reddening. Then he straightened up and took a wristwatch out of the drawer. 'At first glance a perfectly ordinary digital watch,' Z declared. 'But when I hold down these two buttons at the same time...'

Nothing happened.

'Umm . . . no, sorry, not those two, this one and . . . *this* one . . .'

With a fierce hiss a fine red beam of light shot out from the side of the watch and sliced through several flowers that were standing in a vase on the other side of the room. 'An ultra-fine laser beam,' said Z. 'Capable of cutting through reinforced steel' – he glanced across the room – 'and some rather nice chrysanthemums.' He handed the watch across the desk. 'Strap it on, Triple Zero, and, for goodness sake, be careful which buttons you press. One of our top scientists is still looking for his index finger.'

Kip took the watch and removed his own, slipping it into his pocket. Then he gingerly strapped on the new one.

'The watch also has a useful location device built into it,' added Z. 'Which means we can find you wherever you are.' He took a small screen from his pocket and pressed a button. Immediately a red dot illuminated on the screen. 'That's you,' he said helpfully.

'Cool,' said Kip, and Z gave him a quizzical look.

'Now, something else that might prove useful.' Z reached into his inside breast pocket and pulled out a pen. 'Looks like a perfectly ordinary ballpoint, doesn't it? But when I twist the button and press it three times . . .' He looked at it blankly for a moment. 'No, this is *my* pen,' he said. '*This* is perfectly ordinary . . .' He rooted in his pocket and found another one. 'But this one . . . Ah, now *this* one, if I twist the button clockwise and press it three times . . .' He did so and the pen began to flash with a bright red light. 'Excellent. I have just activated an explosive device with enough power to blow this entire room to smithereens. It will go off in exactly sixty seconds . . . unless, of course, I defuse it.'

'How do we do that?' asked Kip nervously.

'Err . . . good question. I simply press the button six times.' Z did that, but the pen continued to flash. 'Or was it seven times?' he murmured. He tried that too but still the pen flashed. Kip stared across the desk open-mouthed, but Z seemed perfectly calm. 'No, no, that's not right, it was definitely six. Ah, I think I remember! I'm supposed to do three, then pause . . . and then do the other three.' He tried that sequence and the flashing stopped. Kip remembered to breathe.

Z twisted the button to its original position and slid it back into his pocket.

'Now then, Triple Zero, pay attention. I—'

'Haven't you forgotten something?' interrupted Kip. Z gave him a blank look. 'The pen?' he added.

'Oh, yes, sorry.' Z pulled out the pen again. 'Put it somewhere safe, and remember, when you want to defuse it, press it three times, *pause*, then do another three – never a straight six. We don't want any accidents, do we?'

Kip took the pen and examined it. It certainly did look very ordinary. 'Brill,' he said, and once again Z stared at him.

'There's one more thing,' Z announced. He pressed yet another button on the desktop and a second secret drawer slid open. He withdrew a tiny black cube the size of a box of matches.

When Kip looked closer he could see that it had a little slider on its top surface. 'What's that?' he asked.

'It's absolutely the latest thing to come off our production line,' announced Z. 'I'm afraid I don't have enough room in here to demonstrate it properly.'

'Yes, but what is it?' repeated Kip.

'It's a six-man tent, complete with emergency rations for two weeks,' said Z.

Kip looked at him. 'Gerraway!' he said.

'I can assure you, I'm not joking,' Z assured him. 'If you need somewhere to shelter, you simply place it on a piece of open ground and activate it.'

'How do I do that?' asked Kip.

'Like so,' said Z placing his finger on the slider and pushing it forward until it clicked. Then he gazed down at it in annoyance. 'Oh, drat!'

The box was already unfolding itself, its base opening out like the petals of a flower, doubling in size and then unfolding and doubling again. As Kip stared incredulously it grew quickly to the size of Z's desk and kept right on going, its outermost edges drooping down onto the floor.

'How do you stop it?' asked Kip.

'You can't,' Z told him. 'So we'll have to be quick.' He managed to open the secret drawer a second time and took out another black cube, which he handed to Kip. 'Put this one somewhere safe,' he said. 'Now, there's no time to waste. We—' He broke off as a wall of green nylon sprouted upwards from the base of the rectangle and guy ropes shot out at forty-five-degree angles, making sounds like whip cracks, each rope ending in a sharp metal spike. They were doubtless intended to embed themselves in soft ground, but here they simply bounced off the tiled floor, in some cases cracking them.

Z reached up and pulled down a sheet of nylon so he could continue talking through the gap. 'We managed to intercept Doctor Kasabian's signal,' he said. 'We traced it to—'

The sheet twanged upwards again, flinging him backwards against a wall. Kip had to duck as another guy rope shot over his head and the peg ricocheted off the wall behind him.

A window in the sheet of nylon unzipped and Z's head reappeared, still talking. '... A volcanic island off the coast of Ecuador! I have a plane standing by to take you there. Your old friend Flight Lieutenant Jimmy Tacklemore will brief you on the way. You—' Tall tent poles suddenly reared up from the desktop and the nylon sheet doubled in height, throwing Z backwards again. There was an interval while he tried to struggle his way around the side of the tent, gasping as he did so. When his face reappeared, his immaculately groomed grey hair was stuck up in all directions as though he'd been electrocuted. 'Your mission, Triple Zero, is to infiltrate Kasabian's hideaway and save the world, by whatever means prove necessary. Good luck!'

Kip opened his mouth to try another excuse but the seat beneath him shuddered as the trap door below it slid silently open and the chair began to sink into the ground. Kip had one last glimpse of Z struggling valiantly to hold back the huge tent that now covered his entire office – then the trapdoor above him slid shut and he was dropping quickly and silently into the earth below.

'*Ecuador!*' said a voice in his ear. '*Beth told me she's in a jungle. I think that might be where she is.*'

'But I thought you said I shouldn't *go* on a mission,' protested Kip, clinging onto his chair. 'You said . . .'

'*That was before I knew your destination. With any luck, the plane will take you straight to Beth. So I think you should go with it.*'

'Do I get a choice?'

There was no answer to that.

After a few moments the chair clanged to a halt with an impact that shook every bone in Kip's body. He looked around in dull amazement. He was in a huge aircraft hangar. All around him fighter planes stood waiting for their latest mission. A man in a pilot's outfit came striding purposefully towards him, his helmet tucked under one arm. He was tall with sharp features and an old-fashioned handlebar moustache. Kip realised this must be the man that Z had just mentioned. He reminded himself that Flight Lieutenant Jimmy Tacklemore was supposed to be an old friend.

'Agent Triple Zero,' the pilot said. 'Jolly good to have you on board, old boy. It's been a long time. I must say, that's an amazing disguise, absolutely amazing!' He helped Kip up out of his seat, spun him round and slipped an arm across his shoulders.

'How are you . . . Jimmy?' murmured Kip.

'I'm splendid, old chap, absolutely raring to go. It's an honour to work with you again. We haven't teamed up since it all kicked off in Libya, have we?'

'Er . . . no, that was . . . fun, wasn't it?'

'Only if you like dodging bullets!' He looked serious for a moment. 'Sorry to hear about your wife, by the way.'

Kip stared at him. This was a surprise. As far as Kip could remember, Corder hadn't been married in the last film, though he had been getting on very well with his female sidekick Agent Triple Three. 'I'm... married?' he whispered.

'Not any more, old boy! Seems like only yesterday we were all standing at the altar. Only time I've ever been asked to be a best man.' He sighed, shook his head. 'Who'd have guessed she'd turn out to be a Russian double agent?'

'Not me,' admitted Kip.

'Still, you soon gave her the old heave-ho, didn't you? Bit of an extreme way to get a divorce but it *was* self-defence!' Tacklemore seemed to dismiss the matter. 'Now, if you'd like to step this way...' He indicated a huge charcoal-grey stealth jet waiting on the Tarmac by the open doors of the hangar. 'Your chariot awaits!'

'Wow!' Kip was trying to think of something to say but the best he could manage was, 'Do I get a window seat?'

The man laughed again, as though Kip had just cracked a really good joke. 'You're a card, Triple Zero. An absolute hoot! The other agents take it all so seriously, but you... you like to have a good laugh! Now, come on, we need to get you to your destination, clickety-click. It's time Doctor Leo

Kasabian learned a valuable lesson – that you can't push the world around without getting slapped in the face – and, by golly, you're just the chap to teach it to him!'

CHAPTER NINE

The Chase

Beth couldn't help herself. She *hated* spiders, and what she did next was just a reflex action. She screamed and kicked her legs to try and shake the spider off. In this she was successful, but the noise of her yell, amplified by the metal tunnel all around her, caused the two uniformed men to spin round and stare through the grille at her.

It also caused Mr Lazarus to start shouting questions into her earpiece. *'Beth! What's wrong? You nearly deafened me. Are you in trouble?'*

There was no time to answer him. Beth started crawling onwards again, moving as quickly as the cramped space would allow. She glanced over her shoulder, and was happy to note that the spider, no doubt more frightened than she was, was scuttling away in the opposite direction. But, at the same instant, there was a loud crash as the metal grille was lifted clear of its opening – then a helmeted head swung into view and a muffled voice yelled at her to come back.

Beth ignored the command and kept going, following the long, straight run of the tunnel; when she looked back a second time she saw that one of the men had climbed in behind her and was coming in pursuit. She snatched a breath and redoubled her efforts, moving as quickly as possible, wincing from the pain in her grazed knees and elbows. Whenever she dared to look behind her it appeared that the man was gaining on her. Though more cramped than she was, his padded suit gave him protection from the hard metal surfaces all around him – and he was clearly intent on catching up with her.

'*Beth, for heaven's sake, what's going on?*'

'Being . . . chased!' she gasped. 'Can't talk now . . .'

'*Chased by whom?*'

'No time . . . to talk about it!'

She kept going until she came to a second ventilation grille. Pausing to have a peep through it, she found herself looking into another underground cavern, but this one appeared to be empty of men and equipment. As far as she could see all it contained was a wide, deep pit of what looked like hot coals – indeed, she could feel the heat of them radiating through the grille onto her sweating face.

The pit extended wall-to-wall, but a narrow stone walkway spanned it and led to a door on the far side: a possible route of escape.

She glanced back again and almost yelled in terror when she saw how close her pursuer was. He had cast off his helmet now, and the expression on his dark, sweating face was not an agreeable one. Beth twisted herself round with great difficulty, until she was able to place her feet against the metal grille, and then she began to pound at it, pulling back her feet and thrusting them forward again, kicking as hard as she could. At first the grille seemed too strong for her to make any impression but, as she continued to kick, it began to give way under the pressure, until finally one corner of it snapped free and it hinged aside. Beth got her legs through the gap and began to edge herself through the opening, then suddenly, heart-stoppingly, a gloved hand reached out and grabbed her by the shoulder. She flung up an arm and, more by accident than design, her fist hit her pursuer full in the face, causing him to give a grunt of pain and let go of her. She wriggled frantically through the opening and dropped the short distance to the ground, reminding herself as she did so that there was a pit of hot coals somewhere out there and it wouldn't be a good idea to fall into it. Her feet thudded onto solid ground a mere centimetre or two from the edge of the pit and a great up-rush of hot air threatened to take off her eyebrows. Beth stood for a moment, waving her arms in a desperate attempt to regain her balance and then steadying herself she began to edge sideways, heading for the spot where the walkway crossed the pit. As she went she noticed a crudely written sign that had been placed at the edge of the pit. *Lake Boasian*.

'Don't be stupid,' snarled a voice from behind her. She looked up to see her pursuer's brooding face, a trickle of blood pulsing from his nose. 'That's molten lava down there. The temperature's more than a thousand degrees centigrade, you'll fry.'

Beth ignored his advice and kept moving sideways until she was level with the walkway. It was disconcertingly narrow, no more than fifteen centimetres wide and, when she looked out towards its centre, she saw, to her alarm, that parts of it had actually crumbled away, leaving no more than a brick's width at its narrowest point. Some six metres below it the surface of the white-hot lava bubbled and steamed.

'Listen to me!' urged the man. 'That thing isn't safe; nobody's used it for years. Now, come back here and give yourself up. We're not going to hurt you. We just want to ask you some questions.'

Beth shook her head. She'd seen enough Corder films to know that questions asked by villains were nearly always accompanied by horrific torture. In the last film, Triple Zero had been tied to a chair and a henchman had pulled his fingernails out with a set of pliers. No, she told herself, she'd be all right, just so long as she didn't look down . . .

'*Beth*,' said the voice in her ear. '*I'm not sure what it is you're doing, but it doesn't sound like it's very safe.*'

'Shush!' she snapped. 'I need to concentrate . . .'

She took a deep breath and started across the pit, holding her arms out by her sides like a tightrope walker.

'It doesn't fit,' said Kip dejectedly.

He was standing in the hold of the stealth bomber currently flying at 40,000 feet and twice the speed of sound – or so Flight Lieutenant Tacklemore had assured him. Kip was wearing a skin-diving outfit over his other clothes, one that had clearly been designed for a much taller man. He was also wearing a leather sheath strapped to his thigh, which contained the biggest knife he'd ever seen – and under the outfit, in a waterproof shoulder holster, a lethal-looking pistol. 'This outfit's way too big,' Kip added, just in case Tacklemore hadn't got the message. 'Look at the legs and arms.'

Tacklemore looked offended. 'You can't blame us, old boy. We had no idea you'd be using such a radical disguise. But, don't worry, that suit is state-of-the-art. Even with the sleeves turned back it won't let a drop of water through.' The pilot frowned. 'Explain to me again how they managed to make you a foot shorter,' he muttered. 'I didn't quite follow you before. You said something about... New tech freaks?'

Kip waved a hand as if to dismiss the idea. 'I can't be bothered with all that... science stuff,' he said. 'It's... dead boring.' He looked down at the flippers on his feet, which were also much too roomy. 'You'd better tell me how all this stuff works,' he said. 'I've never gone skin diving before.'

Tacklemore laughed as though Kip had just

cracked another joke. 'You'll be telling me next you didn't finish top of your class in scuba training!' he said.

Kip laughed along with him. 'Can't get much past you,' he muttered. 'Seriously, though, just . . . remind me. When I get into the water, this thing goes over my face, right?' He indicated the mask that was dangling at his side. 'And these tanks on my back, they feed me the air. But . . . how do I switch 'em on?'

'You know perfectly well these new systems are water-activated.'

Kip forced a laugh. 'Just making sure you're paying attention,' he said. 'OK, so why do I need this outfit? Surely we could just land on the island and—'

'No way, Triple Zero! We have to do this hush-hush, commando style. We'll drop you a half mile offshore and—'

'Drop me?' Kip stared at him aghast.

'By parachute,' said Flight Lieutenant Tacklemore indicating a small pack above the oxygen tanks. 'Our sonar has indicated that there's an underwater entrance and—'

'I have to swim half a mile?' Kip shook his head.

'I'm not being funny, but I haven't even got my hundred metres medal yet.'

'*Stop saying things like that,*' said the voice in his ear. '*Remember, you're a super spy.*'

'Well, I'm sorry but that's a heck of a long way.'

'Who are you talking to?' asked Flight Lieutenant Tacklemore.

'Nobody,' said Kip. He coughed loudly. 'I'm just, er... talking to myself. It's something I do. I find it... relaxes me.' He frowned, made an effort to try and look as though he knew what he was doing. 'Right, so let's get this straight. I jump from the plane, I swim through an underwater tunnel and then...?'

'You'll be met by your contact, Agent Two Seven Zero. As you know, we've managed to smuggle a mole into Kasabian's headquarters...'

'A mole?' Kip stared at him. 'What, you mean...?'

'*Kip, don't say anything stupid!*'

'Oh, sure, a *mole*. A double agent. Yeah, cool,' he recovered.

'After that, it's up to the two of you. You'll take out Doctor Kasabian by whatever means are at your disposal. Obviously we'd prefer him alive but if you're lucky enough to get the blighter in your sights...' Tacklemore drew two fingers into the shape of a gun and blew air out from between his pursed lips, making a sound like a gunshot. 'You know, I envy you.'

'Do you?'

'Yes. What I wouldn't give to be able to take your place.'

'Oh, well, if you really fancy it...'

'But, of course, I couldn't do it half as well as you.'

'No?'

'No. You're the best we have, Triple Zero. When I think of all the amazing things you've done for your country, well...it makes me appreciate the sacrifice you're about to make.'

Kip looked at him uneasily. 'S-sacrifice?' he murmured.

'Why, yes. People tried to warn you this is a suicide mission. They said your chances of survival were a thousand to one, but still you volunteered.'

'*I expect he's exaggerating,*' whispered Mr Lazarus.

'He'd better be,' murmured Kip, and Flight Lieutenant Tacklemore gave him an odd look.

'I say, old boy. Are you all right?'

'I'm ... fine,' whispered Kip. 'I'm great, really, just ... you know how it is. Can't wait to ... get started.'

'Excellent. Well, you may as well make yourself comfortable. We'll be coming up on target in an hour or so. I'll just go and have a quick word with the pilot. It's Billy Frobisher, by the way.'

'Is it really?' said Kip. 'Good old ... Billy! How is he?'

'You can come and have a word in person, if you like.'

'No, I'll ... stay here, thanks. Prepare myself for the mission, and all that. Get myself ... in the zone.'

'Jolly good show, old boy.' Tacklemore started to turn away and then seemed to remember something and turned back. 'I almost forgot.' He pulled a small canister from his pocket and clipped it to a catch on Kip's belt. 'You may need this.'

Kip gazed down at it, mystified. It looked like a small can of air freshener. 'What is it?' he asked.

'Shark repellent,' said Flight Lieutenant Tacklemore. 'Apparently these waters are teeming with the blighters. Just aim for the eyes and press the trigger.' He turned and strode off in the direction of the cabin.

Kip stood there, looking at the small can hanging from his belt. 'Did you hear that?' he snarled. 'Flipping sharks!'

But if Mr Lazarus was still listening, he didn't bother to give an answer.

CHAPTER TEN

The Corder Ultimatum

'Beth, what exactly are you doing?'

Six metres below Beth the molten lava bubbled and hissed, and the heat rising from its surface seemed to envelope her from head to foot, making fresh sweat trickle from every pore.

'Come back,' urged a voice behind her, but it was little more than a whisper now, as though the man was afraid of startling her. 'You'll die out there.'

Beth tried not to think about that and kept going. She made it as far as the centre of the path without too much effort, but then she became aware of just how badly the walkway had eroded out here and, against all her better judgment, she paused to look down. She saw that her ruined shoes were now standing on a piece of stone that was literally crumbling at the edges, the white granite falling as a fine cloud of powder that turned to sparks in the fierce orange heat below. She warned herself not to panic and took another step...

another…and another…And then there was an ominous cracking sound…Looking down again Beth could see that the narrow piece of stone on which she was standing was splintering across the middle, a jagged mark extending slowly from left to right beneath the soles of her shoes.

There was no time to think. She bent her knees, pushed down with her right foot and leaped, a fraction of a second before the stone split in two and fell into the pit. She was left suspended a moment, travelling forward through the air, and then her left foot came down onto stone and she didn't hesitate but began to run, horribly aware as she did so that each piece of stone was breaking away an instant after her foot had lifted from it. For a moment she was convinced that she wasn't going to make it…

But then her right foot finally found purchase on a solid piece of stone and Beth was moving onwards to the far edge of the pit. She stepped onto firm ground and span round to send a triumphant smile back at her pursuer, who was still hanging out of the ventilation shaft, staring across at her in open-mouthed astonishment. She even felt cheered enough to give him a brief wave. As she stood there a last couple of sections broke from the walkway and dropped into the lava, causing a great flash and a cloud of smoke. There was no way anybody was going to follow her across.

Beth turned away and walked the short distance to the metal door. It was only then that it occurred to her that it might be locked, that she might be trapped here until somebody came to fetch her...

But the handle turned easily at her touch and the door swung silently open...

And a man was staring down at her: a huge man, a man so tall that he would have had to stoop to get under the lintel of the door. He had a brutish, ape-like face, thick wiry hair that stuck up from his scalp in tufts, and when he grinned down at her he displayed two rows of misshapen yellow teeth.

Beth stooped to try and scoot past him but he was too quick for her. A hand the size of a joint of beef grabbed her under the arm, and before she knew what was happening she'd been swept up into the man's arms and he was carrying her, kicking and struggling down the corridor beyond.

'Let me go!' she squealed. 'Put me down right now, you big oaf!'

'*Beth, what's going on?*'

'I've been grabbed by a . . . An apeman!'

The man just laughed, a strange snuffling laugh that made him appear even more ape-like than before. He seemed to know exactly where he was going, twisting left and right along a labyrinth of underground tunnels until finally he reached a metal door, which slid open at his approach. He carried Beth into a huge circular room that was, for the moment, in darkness. He walked to the centre of the room and dumped her into a black leather chair. The instant she dropped into it metal bracelets that were mounted in the arms and legs of the chair clamped themselves automatically around her wrists and ankles, holding her firmly in position. The big man grunted with satisfaction, then stepped back from the chair and seemed to melt into the surrounding darkness. There was a brief silence.

Suddenly a powerful spotlight clicked on, directing a blinding glare straight into her eyes. Beth blinked and gazed helplessly around but she could see nothing other than smooth steel walls curving about her. She waited. After a few more minutes another figure stepped out of the shadows, a tall, wiry woman dressed in some kind of dark brown uniform – a shirt, a pair of jodhpurs and long leather boots. Her blonde hair was tied up on top of her head in a complicated series of knots, and her thin mouth was inexpertly painted with bright red lipstick. Beth noticed, with a sinking feeling deep inside, that the woman was carrying a leather riding crop in one gloved hand.

Her thin lips twisted themselves into an unpleasant smirk. 'So,' she said, in a strangely accented purr. 'It would appear that we have an unexpected visitor.' She leaned closer and studied Beth with cold green eyes. 'You are in trouble, kitten. Big trouble. If you want to live, I would advise you to tell me everything you know.'

Jason Corder was absolutely furious. He had just woken up in a grubby corridor to discover that there was a nasty cut over his left eye, his body ached in half a dozen places and, worst of all, his favourite grey suit was torn at one shoulder. He had been professionally ambushed, but by who and why, he had no idea. When he stormed into Z's office he found his familiar contact kneeling on the floor, carefully folding what looked like a large green tent. Z glanced up from his work and for a moment his blue eyes widened in recognition – then they narrowed suspiciously as they took in Corder's bruised face and bedraggled appearance.

'Who the hell are you?' he asked.

Corder glared down at him in disbelief.

'Who do you think I am, you idiot? We had an appointment. You were going to brief me for the latest mission . . .'

Z frowned, shook his head. 'You certainly *look* like Corder,' he admitted. 'But you can't be him, can you, since I've just finished briefing the *real* Triple Zero?'

'What are you blathering about?' Corder wondered if his handler was going mad. Half an hour ago everything had seemed normal. He'd been on his way to the briefing when suddenly, out of thin air, he'd been struck in the back. The last thing he remembered was lurching towards that flight of stairs. Then a series of fireworks had gone off in his head and, the next thing he knew, he'd come to his senses lying in a dark corner, his head throbbing. 'Somebody jumped me out there,' he said. 'I've only just woken up.' He indicated the cut on his forehead. 'Look at the state of me.'

Z abandoned his tent-folding duties and got to

his feet. 'You expect me to believe that?' he laughed. 'I'll admit they've done a good job on you. But they haven't quite got the eyes right.'

'The eyes?' Corder moved closer to Z. 'I haven't the faintest idea what you're on about. Of course I'm me. Look at me, for goodness sake! We've been doing missions together for years.'

Z nodded. 'You can't fool me. The real Corder was in here only half an hour ago. Of course, he was disguised as a twelve-year-old boy, but—'

'Have you gone barmy?' growled Corder. 'How is such a thing possible?'

Z tapped the side of his nose. 'Department seventeen,' he murmured. 'New tech freaks. I suppose you've got a similar team working for your side, the ones who made you look like Corder?'

'*My* side? You bloody idiot. I'm with MI6! You've sent an imposter on my mission!'

'Nonsense. It was Corder. Had to be. His ID matched perfectly.' Z held out his hand. 'If you're who you claim to be you'll have some ID too.'

'Of course!' Corder reached into his inside pocket and gave a gasp of surprise when he realised the card wasn't there. 'I've been robbed!' he said. 'Somebody's taken it.'

'Oh, very convincing,' sneered Z. 'Is that the best you can do? You'll be telling me next that I've sent a genuine twelve-year-old boy on a highly dangerous mission...' His voice trailed away and a flicker of doubt flared in his eyes. 'Mind you,' he murmured. 'He didn't seem to be taking the role very seriously. I told him off about it once or twice.'

'You fool! Tell me I'm dreaming this.' Corder looked around the office, weighing up his best course of action. 'Well, one thing's for sure, whoever he was, I've got to go after him ASAP. You'd better send me down to the hangars and tell them to have a plane ready for immediate takeoff. If I can get straight on his tail...'

But Z was shaking his head. 'Not so fast,' he said. 'Your story sounds plausible but I'm not so stupid as to allow you access to our hangars. For all I know you could be a foreign agent trying to bluff your way down there. Oh, you'd love that, wouldn't you? A chance to study all our latest kit up close. Who knows what havoc you could wreak? No, first we'll have to establish your identity using old-fashioned face recognition and DNA technology. If everything checks out *then* we'll send you on your way.'

'How long will that take?'

'We should have a definitive answer in three or four hours.'

Corder shook his head. 'There isn't time,' he protested. 'I need to get straight after him, whoever he is. You said he was a . . . kid?'

'Umm. No, I said he was an agent *disguised* as a kid. Quite the most amazing transformation I've ever seen . . .' Again doubt flickered in Z's eyes. 'I did wonder how they'd managed to make him a foot shorter . . .'

Corder groaned. 'This is unbelievable,' he muttered. 'When all this is over, I'll be recommending you for early retirement. You've obviously lost your marbles.' The spy moved to the desk and punched a button, bringing the chair up from below floor level. 'What plane was he travelling in?'

'The, er . . . X Nineteen stealth fighter,' muttered Z.

'The—?' Corder had heard everything now. 'Let's get this straight. You've put a twelve-year-old kid aboard the fastest spy plane in the world?'

'Of course not! I mean, he's not a kid! He certainly *looks* like one, but, as far as I'm aware he's, er . . . well, he's you.'

'I see. And if he's me, then who am I?'

105

'You're er…somebody else. Obviously. Until proved otherwise.'

'Right. And once you've established my true identity, how would you suggest I catch up with this…imposter?'

'There's a very nice X Seven down there,' said Z. 'On a good day it can do at least…ooh, a third of the X Nineteen's speed.' He took a small screen from his pocket. 'He's also wearing a trackable watch so it'll be a simple enough matter to follow him.'

'Oh, well, that's OK then,' said Corder. 'For a minute there I thought we were in trouble.' He pondered briefly and then shook his head. 'There's no time to waste,' he decided. 'Protocol will have to wait.' He started towards the chair. 'If I can just get after him, there's a chance we—'

'Hold it right there,' growled Z, and a sudden hard edge in his voice warned Corder to stop and turn round. He saw that Z had taken an umbrella from a nearby stand and was pointing it at him, holding it like a rifle. 'I'm sorry,' he said. 'But until we've established your identity I simply cannot allow you to leave. Now, you're going to stay right where you are, while I summon help.'

Corder smirked. 'An umbrella?'

'It may *look* like a perfectly ordinary umbrella, but when I press this button here...' There was a hiss, and a brightly coloured dart shot out of the handle of the umbrella and thudded into Z's chest. He looked down at it in mild surprise. 'Wrong way round,' he croaked, and then crumpled silently to the floor. Corder didn't hesitate. He stepped forward, checked that Z was breathing and moved him into the recovery position. He searched his handler's pockets, pulling out his identity card and the small tracking screen. He transferred the items to his own pockets. Then turning away he hurried back to the desk, punched a button and flung himself into the chair as it began to descend.

As the chair dropped silently down the vertical shaft he thought furiously. The other agent would have a pretty good head start but Corder could easily track him to his destination, and hopefully he'd get there in time to stop him from making a mess of this all-important mission. The only thing was, who *was* he? And how had he managed to infiltrate a top-secret organisation without being caught?

When the chair finally came to a halt he sprang out of it and strode towards a surprised-looking member of flight crew who was enjoying a sneaky cup of coffee.

'You!' snapped Corder, waving Z's ID card at the man. 'This is an emergency. Get me a pilot and your fastest plane prepped for takeoff immediately.'

'Yes, *sir*!' The crewman dropped the coffee and hurried to organise things.

Meanwhile Corder took the screen from his pocket and pressed the button. The screen lit up with a map of the world and a small flashing red spot, which indicated that his quarry was already hundreds of miles away, heading east.

'What's your game?' whispered Corder fiercely. 'What are you up to? Whatever it is, I'll find you. That's a promise. And when I do . . .' He drew his fingers into the shape of a gun and blew out from between his pursed lips, making a sound like gunfire.

Mr Lazarus took a sharp intake of breath. Kip's on-screen progress had been interrupted by an unexpected scene featuring Jason Corder. The world's most dangerous secret agent had just sworn bloody vengeance on a twelve-year-old boy; Mr Lazarus realised that everything had gone too far. As if things weren't bad enough Kip would now have a highly trained killer on his tail. Mr Lazarus knew that he had to help the boy. But how could he be expected to do that when he was stuck here in the projection room?

He realised that there was only one choice left to him. It was against all the rules of caution and logic, and he knew that it could go horribly wrong – he also silently cursed the fact that, in all the years since its invention, he had somehow never got around to making another Retriever. It would have been a very handy thing to have right now. But Kip had the only one in existence, and he was stuck in the film – it was up to Mr Lazarus to do something to help.

He walked quickly to the door of the projection room and turned the key in the lock. He couldn't afford to have somebody come in and tamper with the running projector while he was gone. He cast a quick glance over the machinery, ensuring that there was nothing that could go wrong. Then he moved back to stand beside the Enigma and placed one foot on the wooden platform. He stood, poised, his head turned to one side so he could see through the viewing window to the flickering images on the screen in the auditorium. He was waiting. Waiting for the right moment to go into the film . . .

CHAPTER ELEVEN

Splashdown

'Get yourself ready,' said Flight Lieutenant Tacklemore giving Kip a cheery thumbs up. He had one hand on Kip's shoulder and was guiding him forward, towards the open door of the stealth plane.

'Look, can we talk about this?' muttered Kip. 'I have to tell you, I'm not feeling good about it. I . . . I have this problem with diving . . .'

This was absolutely true. Kip was thinking about his swimming lessons back in the real world. They were held at the local pool, once a week. He was a pretty poor swimmer, but was always prepared to give it his best effort. When it came to diving, that was another matter. His PE instructor, Mr Davies, a big brutish Welshman, couldn't seem to understand the problem at all. He'd stand at the side of the pool in his ill-fitting, bright yellow tracksuit, staring impatiently up at Kip as he shivered on the diving board, desperately trying to work up enough nerve to take the plunge. But he just couldn't seem to do it. Time and again he would be on the point of throwing himself off and something would stop him. He would stand there in absolute humiliation, painfully aware of the other pupils sniggering at him and whispering to each other. He would stare down into the clear, rippling depths of the pool, and Kip didn't know what it was he was afraid of, but he *was* afraid, afraid to just push off with his toes and let himself go . . .

And now here he stood on the bay of a stealth plane, and he was having exactly the same feelings, except this was infinitely worse because, when he finally edged close enough to see out of the door, the raging wind whipping at his face and hair, Kip realised that he would be jumping into almost total darkness. A terrible, paralysing fear seemed to ebb through his entire body and he knew that he would never be able to do this, not in a million years.

Flight Lieutenant Tacklemore indicated a small red bulb above the door. 'When that turns amber,' he shouted above the rush of wind, 'you get yourself ready – and when it turns green, you jump! It'll be dark down there, so don't forget you've a powerful light on top of your face mask. The switch is right here.' He tapped the side of Kip's head.

'I'm...not really feeling all that well,' protested Kip. 'I wonder if maybe we should head back and try again tomorrow?'

'Nonsense, Triple Zero!' yelled Flight Lieutenant Tacklemore. 'There's no time to waste. Goodness me, this is nothing to a man like you! What about all the amazing stunts you've pulled off over the years? Like in Egypt when you drove a car out of the skyscraper and into the side of a helicopter? Or in Russia where you abseiled upside down from a plane holding a nuclear device...and you still managed to shoot thirty-one of the blighters on the way down? It's a wonder you survived either of those stunts. But here you are, alive and kicking! This is, if you'll forgive the pun, just a drop in the ocean.'

'Yes, but—'

'You're a highly trained super agent. There's nobody else like you in the world.'

The bulb turned amber and Flight Lieutenant Tacklemore edged Kip even closer to the open doorway.

'It's just...it's just that I...need a little more time to think about it,' croaked Kip. He could feel a terrible turbulence in his stomach and half expected to throw up at any moment, which was something he'd never seen Corder do. 'You know, I'm sure I'm coming down with a throat infection. I feel really dodgy.'

'Just think about all the people who are depending on you!' roared Tacklemore. 'You don't want to let them down, do you?'

'Well, I—'

'You're their last hope, Triple Zero. You can't give up now. You just can't.'

'Well, OK, but all I'm saying is, can we please slow things down a bit? See, I need to be—'

Kip was still mid-sentence when two things happened in quick succession. The light bulb turned green and Flight Lieutenant Tacklemore gave him a hard shove in the back. And then, suddenly, horribly, he was out of the plane and falling through empty air, his body twisting and turning as he fell.

For a moment there was nothing, so deep was his shock. Then a million thoughts came racing into his head all at the same time, an unintelligible jumble of ideas and suggestions that were tumbling over each other in their haste to make themselves known.

OhmigodI'mfallingwhatamIgoingtodoIwishIwasstill-athomeamIgoingtodie?

And then a calm voice cut through everything else.

'*Kip, don't panic.*'

'I'm falling!' cried Kip, and his voice was almost swept away on the rush of wind blasting by him. 'I'm falling out of the plane! I was *pushed*!'

'*I know, I can see you. I think the Flight Lieutenant said something about a parachute.*'

'Yes, yes, that's right! He did! But...I don't know how to open it!'

'*Look for the ripcord.*'

'What's that?'

'*It's a handle you pull that opens the parachute.*'

Kip groped frantically at his chest, trying to find anything that felt like a handle, but he came up empty. As his body twisted round he caught a glimpse of a flat darkness below him and realised that this must be the water, coming at him much too fast.

'There's no handle!' he gasped.

'*A button then? Something you hit with your hand?*'

Kip groped at his chest again and realised that a pack strapped to his chest had a large rubber button on the front of it. He lifted a fist and bought it down hard on the button. Almost instantly there was a swishing sound and his downward momentum was abruptly slowed as something above him filled with air, the resistance wrenching every muscle in his body. He was now descending at a much slower rate.

'I did it,' he gasped. 'It opened, Mr Lazarus!'

'*Good boy. Now listen to me, I'm coming in . . .*'

But at that instant Kip's legs hit the water. He went under the surface and gasped at how cold the sea was. He gulped down a mouthful of salty water then coughed it out. He remembered the face mask and groped for it, pulled it on, but it was full of water and for a moment he panicked, starting to thrash around like a drowning man . . . Then a distant memory came to him, somebody on a snorkeling holiday in Spain telling him that you had to blow the water out of the mask before you could start breathing. He tried that, coughing and spluttering like a walrus, before the oxygen mixture filled his mouth and nose and he was able to breathe again. He reached the end of his descent and began to rise in the water. He surfaced under the tangled silk of his parachute and spent quite a bit of time flailing like an idiot as he tried to free himself from the various ropes and strings, before remembering the large knife he carried in the scabbard strapped to his thigh. He pulled out the knife and slashed at the ropes, cutting through them easily. Then he ducked under the parachute and swam a short distance away from it.

Kip surfaced and bobbed in the water for a moment, looking around, trying to calm himself. At first he saw nothing but darkness in every direction but then his eyes made out the occasional flash of a distant light ahead of him and he realised this must be the island he was looking for. Flight Lieutenant Tacklemore had said something about it being half a mile away but to his inexperienced eyes it looked a lot further than that.

'Everything all right?'

Kip had half expected the Communicator to fail once it hit the water, but this new model seemed to be able to handle it fine. Kip trod water while he lifted the mask from his face so he could reply. 'I'm alive, at any rate,' he spluttered. 'I have to try and get to the island. I won't be able to talk to you while I'm swimming.'

'That's probably just as well. Listen, Kip, I'm going to come into the movie.'

'What? But... you never do that!'

'There's a first time for everything. I'm standing here watching the screen, waiting for the right moment. You know how it is. You catch glimpses of people flashing by. And, Kip, I saw a scene a few moments ago . . .'

'Yes?'

'Jason Corder is coming after you.'

'What?' Kip didn't like the sound of that at all. 'But he's a cold-blooded killer, Mr L!'

'I know that. I'm going to try and pick a scene where I can talk to him man to man. I feel sure I can put in a good word for you, persuade him you're no danger to him. But, listen, you realise, don't you, there's only one Retriever? You'll have to wait until Beth and I are with you before you press eject.'

'Right. How *is* Beth?'

'She's in big trouble. I need to get back to her before I come in.'

'What kind of trouble?' asked Kip, but he received no answer to that. Mr Lazarus had switched channels again.

Kip sighed. He slid the knife back into its sheath, then ducked below the surface and began to swim, using the flippers to power himself along. It took him a little while to get the hang of it but, after fifteen minutes or so, he was moving along quite nicely, finding it far easier than relying on his own feet. His anxiety began to ease and he actually found himself wishing that Mr Davies could see him. He wouldn't be quite so quick to make fun now, would he? After all, Kip had dived out of a plane, he'd made a descent by parachute and now he was swimming through shark-infested waters . . .

That last bit stopped him from feeling quite so pleased with himself. He looked nervously this way and that through the dark ocean, but he couldn't see far in any direction. Then he remembered that he had a torch with him, mounted on the top of his face mask; Flight Lieutenant Tacklemore had reminded him about it. Kip reached up a hand and fiddled with the switch, and suddenly a powerful beam knifed through the water ahead of him, lighting up the way for some distance.

And that was when he saw the big, white shape moving towards him at speed – a big white shape with dead, black eyes and a gaping mouth bristling with jagged teeth. Kip's blood seemed to turn to ice in his veins. It was the biggest shark he had ever seen and it was coming straight at him.

***

Beth gazed up into the merciless face that smiled coldly down at her and wondered what she was supposed to say. The woman asking the questions was quite evidently a nasty piece of work – and that wasn't just a reference to her hideous hair and make-up. But what was Beth supposed to do in circumstances like this? Invent a character for herself? Or simply tell the truth? After some consideration she decided to go with the latter idea.

'My name's Beth Slater,' she said, trying to remain calm. 'And I'm ... kind of lost.'

The woman seemed to find this amusing. 'You sound English,' she said. 'So I am guessing you are with MI6, yes?'

'Oh, no,' Beth assured her. 'No, St Thomas's High in Manchester. Do you know it? Terrible place, too much homework. What sort of accent is yours, by the way? You sound Russian or something.'

'My name is Olga. Olga Katamowski.' She leaned closer. 'And I will ask the questions. Now, tell me how you got here.'

'It's going to sound a bit far-fetched...'

'Try me, kitten.'

'Well, I was at the pictures watching this film and—'

'*Don't tell her that!*' whispered Mr Lazarus in Beth's ear. '*Film people don't like to be told they don't really exist. It drives them crazy.*'

'Oh, er…yes, I was watching this film on…on board an aeroplane? Anyway, I decided to go to the toilet and I opened what I thought was the toilet door and it was actually, like, the…the door of the plane…and I fell out…and landed in some bushes.'

Olga took a step back and stood there, her hands on her skinny hips, shaking her head. 'Pathetic,' she sneered. 'That's the best you can do? You fell out of a plane? You'd have been killed.'

'Well, you'd have thought so,' agreed Beth. 'But I crashed through all these leaves and bushes and stuff. Check out my arms, they're cut to ribbons.'

'Hmph!' Olga stepped closer again and studied the wounds. 'You *do* look a little scarred,' she admitted. 'But I don't know. Where were you going on this…plane?'

'Erm…to…Benidorm,' said Beth, naming the only place she had ever flown in her life.

'*Ecuador!*' hissed a voice in her ear.

'To visit my cousin, Benny Dorm, in Ecuador,' she corrected herself.

'I see. It all sounds highly unlikely to me.'

'But not impossible,' rumbled a deep male voice, so amplified it seemed to fill the entire room. Beth looked around to try and see who was speaking but she could see nobody. 'During the Second World War a tail gunner in the Royal Air Force fell eighteen thousand feet from a plane and only suffered a fractured ankle. His fall was broken by pine trees and a fresh layer of snow.'

Olga sneered. 'I didn't say it was impossible,' she muttered. 'Just highly unlikely.'

'The question is, what was she doing crossing Lake Boasian? Does she know anything about its secrets?'

Olga studied Beth for a moment. 'There's only one way to find out,' she said.

There was a long silence, then the deep voice said, 'Torture.'

This was what Beth had been dreading. 'Now, hang on a minute!' she cried. 'There's no need for any unpleasantness. I've told you what happened, can't we just leave it at that?'

Olga shook her head. 'No, we can't.' She kneeled in front of Beth's chair and began removing her shoes.

'What are you doing?' gasped Beth.

'What does it look like?'

'She's taking my shoes off!' cried Beth, more for Mr Lazarus's benefit than anyone else's. 'She's going to torture me! There must be something we can do to stop her!'

Olga gave her a puzzled look. 'Who are you talking to?' she snapped.

'Nobody. Nobody at all. Oh my God, what am I going to do?'

Now Olga was tearing the remains of Beth's tattered tights to reveal her bare feet.

'*Stay calm,*' whispered the voice in her ear.

'That's easy for you to say,' snarled Beth.

'What's easy for me to say?' muttered Olga.

'Umm . . . something in Russian,' said Beth. 'Look, honestly, there really is no need to do anything drastic. I've told you all I know, so, please, just let me—' She broke off as Olga turned aside and reached for something on a low table in the shadows to her left. When she turned back the woman was holding an object in her right hand.

'Wh-what's that?' gasped Beth.

'This is the Truthmaker,' whispered Olga, her eyes flashing maniacally. 'Once I apply this, you will tell me everything you know.'

'But it...it's a feather,' gasped Beth. 'I don't understand.'

'*I suppose it's the 'Twelve' certificate,*' said the voice in her ear. '*They aren't allowed to make things too nasty.*'

'Yes, but, honestly, a feather? That can't—' Beth broke off in surprise. 'Ooh,' she said. 'Stop that! That's 'orrible, that is! Stop it!'

'I'll stop when you've told me the truth,' said Olga calmly. She was applying the tip of the feather to the sole of Beth's left foot, turning it around and around in a tight circular motion. Beth arched herself in the chair, but the manacles prevented her from moving, and the awful, maddening, tickling sensation seemed to be spreading through her entire foot.

'Stop!' she begged. 'Please stop!'

'Not till you tell me,' said Olga. 'I can go on doing this all day if I have to.'

'No, please, please. I . . . I . . .'

'*Don't tell them, Beth!*'

'I have to!'

'*You mustn't!*'

But she couldn't help herself. Suddenly the words were tumbling over each other in their haste to escape from her mouth. 'My friend Kip . . . his dad has a cinema . . . *Arrghh*, stop! And there's a project-ionist there called Mr . . . oh! Mr Lazarus. He's invented this gadget that can put people into films . . . and oh, please! He sent us in here to get an ID card! You're not real! You're fictional. You're just a character in the film, *Spy Another Day*!'

Olga stopped tickling. She looked up at Beth in disgust. 'What are you babbling about?' she said.

'She's clearly quite mad,' boomed the deep voice. 'I'm afraid you won't get anything useful out of her.'

Olga nodded, rather sadly Beth thought. She got back to her feet and returned the feather to its place on the table. Then she clapped her hands together. 'Simeon!' she barked, and the huge, ape-like man came shuffling out of the shadows. The cuffs securing Beth's wrists and ankles slid silently aside and the creature snatched her up in his arms again. 'Take her to the dungeons,' commanded Olga. 'Until we decide what's to be done with her.'

'She might make a suitable candidate for one of my anthropological experiments,' boomed the deep voice.

And with that, Beth was swept out of the room and propelled along a labyrinth of stone corridors before finally being carried into a dark, damp, filthy dungeon. A lock was turned on a steel-barred doorway and Beth was unceremoniously dumped onto a pile of straw. Then the door clanged shut again, the key turned in the lock and she lay there in the half-darkness, thinking that here was another fine mess Mr Lazarus had gotten her into.

And then she nearly jumped out of her skin as a voice beside her said, 'I don't suppose you got any food on you?'

CHAPTER TWELVE

Shark Attack

For an instant Kip froze. He stared aghast into the beam of the torch and at the great, white, open-mouthed creature that was scything through the water towards him, and he thought he was going to die of fright. Then a voice in his ear jerked him back to reality.

'Kip, you've gone very quiet, is everything OK?'

Kip tried to answer and managed to get out one gulped word. 'Shark!' he gasped, and his face mask filled with bubbles. He had to blow hard so he could see again but, when he could, he wished he hadn't bothered. The shark was coming at him like an express train. He remembered the can of repellent that Tacklemore had given him and reached his free hand down to his belt to grope for it. But fear made him clumsy and, as he fumbled it from its catch, it slipped out of his grasp and went whirling down into the depths.

Kip stared after it, torn between going in pursuit or staying where he was.

'Did you say "shark", Kip?' Mr Lazarus sounded annoyingly calm. *'I can't see you right now, but I seem to remember reading that if a shark comes at you the best thing to do is to punch it on the nose.'*

Kip looked up again, the shark was terrifyingly close, close enough for him to see the rows of razor-sharp teeth protruding from its open mouth and the light of his own torch reflecting in those soulless black eyes. He was now able to appreciate how big the creature was: the size of your average truck. Kip seriously doubted that a punch would have any effect whatsoever, except to make it angry – but he dutifully bunched his right hand into a fist and told himself that he would have to give it a try. What other option did he have? He fumbled for the knife and registered with a sense of dull surprise that the sheath strapped to his thigh was empty. When he thought he'd sheathed the knife, he must have missed it completely. For an instant, all hope left him and Kip resigned himself to a horrible death.

And then he remembered the watch that Z had given him and fresh hope flared within him. He lifted his left arm and peered at the various buttons in the glow of his torch, trying to remember which two he was supposed to press.

He became aware of more movement out in the water and, glancing up again, he saw to his horror that two more sharks were approaching from out of the gloom, one to his left, one to his right, while the first one, now dead ahead of him, was moving in for the kill, its wide mouth curving into what looked like a hideous grin of anticipation. There was no more time to waste. Kip extended his left arm to point at the shark then reached up his other hand and began to prod frantically at the buttons.

At first absolutely nothing happened, but he kept going, hitting buttons at random, the shark's great white carcass blotting out everything else in his vision. In a few seconds, he would be dead meat...

'Of course, not all species of shark are dangerous,' said Mr Lazarus. 'In fact most of them are perfectly docile...'

The voice wittered away in the background as Kip struggled maniacally with the buttons. Then suddenly, miraculously, a straight line of neon-red light shot out of the watch and lanced through the water. Startled, the shark tried to veer away, but the beam caught one of its pelvic fins, slicing it clear off and sending a thin trail of blood jetting into the water. Its balance lost, the shark began to spin crazily around on itself as it shot past Kip, its tail swishing. Kip turned back to face the other two sharks but was surprised to see that they too were veering aside, following the same course as the first shark. Lured by its blood, they had decided to go for easier prey.

Kip didn't hang around to watch what followed. It was going to be messy and he didn't want to discover that, once they'd finished their dinner, the sharks were still hungry – so he kicked his legs and continued on his way, powering himself along with as much speed as he could muster. After a short while his legs were killing him, his energy flagging, but he didn't dare stop to rest. He kept right on going until the powerful beam of his torch began to pick out the seaweed-encrusted surface of a sheer cliff rising in front of him, and he reminded himself that he was supposed to be searching for an entrance down here.

'Kip, is everything all right? Why don't you answer me?'

He swam onwards until he was just a short distance from the rock and then, glancing left and right, he realised he didn't know which way to go.

He began to swim to his right, letting the torch beam play over the rock, searching for openings in the stone. He had expected something small and insubstantial, a natural breach in the cliff face – but when he came upon a perfectly circular hatch set into the rock he was pretty sure he'd found what he was looking for. Short of having the words SECRET ENTRANCE written over it, it couldn't have been easier to spot, but then, he reminded himself, villains in Jason Corder films were never very good at keeping a low profile.

He swam up to the entrance and allowed his torch beam to shine along the length of the tunnel. Apart from a few tropical fish and the occasional crab scuttling along the floor, it looked harmless enough. He was about to go in, but some sixth sense made him glance over his shoulder, and that was when he saw the shark rocketing towards him at terrifying speed. There was no time to think. He bundled himself into the opening, and an instant later the shark's nose butted him and he went tumbling head over heels along the tunnel. Kip came to a halt and twisted defensively round, reaching a hand to his watch, but then he saw that the shark had somehow jammed tight in the mouth of the tunnel and was struggling to extricate itself, its mouth gaping and chomping on nothing. Kip thought about giving it a blast from his watch but there seemed to be no point. It was stuck, unable to move in any direction.

Remembering to breathe, Kip turned away and swam along the passage, staring into the beam of the torch. After he had travelled almost thirty metres or so the tunnel ended in a solid wall, but a faint light from above indicated the way to go. He surfaced cautiously and trod water for a while as he gazed around.

He was in a small underground chamber, the walls carved out of solid rock. Kip had surfaced in a circular pool, to one side of which was a changing area, where he could see scuba-diving gear hanging on a series of pegs. He had a good look around to ensure the place was deserted, then swam to the edge of the pool and clambered gratefully out. He took off his mask, undid the harness that held his oxygen tanks in position and lowered them to the ground. Then he pulled open the Velcro fastening on his wet suit and stepped out of it. He saw, to his amazement, that despite being way too big for him the suit had actually done its job perfectly, just as Tacklemore had promised. His clothing was completely dry. He pulled the Retriever from under his shirt and glanced at it doubtfully but the red light under the eject button was still pulsing rhythmically and he had to assume it was still working. He slipped it back into place.

'*Mr Lazarus, are you there?*' he asked.

No answer. Typical. You couldn't shut the old fool up ten minutes ago when Kip had been unable to reply. He wondered if the projectionist had found the right place to enter the film. Or maybe he was talking to Beth right now. Kip remembered telling him that it would be more useful if he could listen to both channels at once.

He stood for a moment, taking stock of his situation. Against all the odds, he had managed to infiltrate Kasabian's hideaway. He found himself wishing that Beth could have seen him fighting his way in here past three ravenous sharks, but he supposed that wasn't really the point. She must be here somewhere and it was his job to find her.

He froze as a door at the far end of the room swung open and a figure, dressed from head to foot in a white overall and wearing a smoked-glass helmet, stepped into the room and strode purposefully towards him. Unsure of what to do, he glanced frantically this way and that, searching for a weapon. Kip noticed a spear gun standing beside the rows of scuba gear and, running to it, he snatched it up and aimed it towards the figure.

'Stay where you are,' he snapped, and had to steel himself from adding the word, *Please*. The figure halted and lifted gloved hands to remove the helmet. Kip couldn't prevent himself from letting out a gasp of astonishment. The face belonged to a woman – and a very beautiful one at that. It was the actress, Jemima Kensington, whom Kip had seen in other films and whom he'd forgotten had a role in this one, even though she'd been right there on the poster back at the Paramount. He'd had a bit of a thing for Jemima ever since he'd seen her in the *St Bunion's* movies. She gazed at him with those incredible turquoise eyes and her red lips curved into an enchanting smile.

'Agent Triple Zero?' she murmured.

The sound of her husky voice made him flinch, so much so that his finger twitched on the trigger of the spear gun. There was a swish, and the deadly spear blurred across the room, missing Jemima's left shoulder by centimetres, tearing out a lock of her auburn hair and burying itself in the wall behind her. She barely flinched.

'That's a nice welcome.' She prowled towards him, her hands on her hips. 'I must say, I expected somebody a little older.'

'I . . . it's a disguise,' squeaked Kip. 'Department seventeen. New tech freaks.' He gestured towards the spear in the wall. 'I'm really sorry, I didn't mean to . . .'

'Don't worry,' she assured him. 'I know your reputation, Triple Zero. You were just showing me your prowess with a spear gun. If you'd have meant to hit me, you would have.' She placed a hand on his shoulder. 'Thank goodness you're here. It's all kicking off and we really don't have time to mess around.' She studied him with a look that made him quiver. 'A pity. Perhaps when it's all over, and you've resumed your more usual look, we'll have time to get . . . better acquainted.'

Kip swallowed nervously. 'Umm . . . that would be . . . nice,' he croaked. He dropped the spear gun. 'So, er . . . you must be the mole that Z was going on about?'

She nodded.

'I've only been here twenty-four hours myself.

Came in a miniature submarine, disguised as a white shark. These waters are teeming with them.'

'Tell me about it! So...er, what's happening here then, Jemima?'

She gave him an odd look.

'Jemima?' she echoed.

Kip cursed his stupidity. Of course, she was no longer Jemima Kensington the actress. Thanks to the Lazarus Enigma she was now actually a real secret agent.

'Sorry, Two Zero Seven...' he remembered.

'Two Seven *Zero*,' she corrected him.

'Yes, it's just this thing I do. I call all my female sidekicks Jemima. After my... my... grandmother.'

'How interesting. Well, let's dispense with the formalities, shall we? I'll call you Jason...and you can call me Kitty.'

'Kitty?'

'Kitty Velour,' she said, and Kip had to work hard not to wince. He knew it was a tradition in these films to give the female characters stupid names, but this had to be the worst ever. She sounded like an air freshener or something.

'Well, then, er...Kitty, perhaps you can...brief me on what's been happening?'

She nodded. 'Kasabian is all set to unleash The Annihilator in' – she glanced at her watch – 'twelve hours and twenty-two minutes. So we need to find our way to his inner sanctum.'

'His what?'

'His secret lair.'

'Oh, but . . .' Kip gestured around him. 'I thought we were already in it.'

Kitty shook her auburn curls. 'We're in his secret hideout, but I'm talking about his own personal space,' she explained. 'You must understand, Kasabian is incredibly secretive. He doesn't let anybody see his face, except for his Russian assistant, Olga Katamowski.'

Kip tried not to laugh.

'That's really her name?' he cried.

'Yes . . . why? What's so funny about it?'

'Er, nothing,' said Kip hastily. *Especially when your name's Kitty Velour*, he thought.

'Of course, we all hear his voice,' continued Kitty. 'It booms around this place night and day, giving orders. We also know about the horrible anthropological experiments he carries out.'

'Experiments? Oh, you mean the rhino sapiens?'

'It's not just them. They're his new project, but he's been trying to splice human genes with those of various animals for years, with varying degrees of success. There's one guy who works for him, they call him Simeon, he's more gorilla than man. And I've heard rumours of other creatures, failed experiments, that are mostly kept down in his laboratory on one of the lower levels. One thing's for certain: Kasabian's a madman and he won't be happy until he's plunged the entire world into chaos.'

Kip sighed. 'Why do they always want to do that?' he muttered.

Kitty stared at him. 'What do you mean?' she asked him.

'The villains in these fi— In these . . . situations, they always want to mess everything up. But, why? What's in it for them?'

'I guess it's just a power thing,' said Kitty. 'Kasabian wants to rule the world and he won't be happy till he achieves that.'

'Ah, well, no use trying to change the script,' said Kip. 'What happens now?'

Kitty walked across to a row of lockers and, opening one of them, she pulled out a white overall like the one she was wearing. 'I left this here for you,' she said. She looked at it doubtfully. 'I *was* expecting somebody a little bigger.'

'Don't worry, I'm getting used to it,' Kip assured her. He took the suit from her and began to struggle into it. He found that if he turned up the legs and arms, he could just about get away with it, though he was sure he must look pretty clownish. 'How is it?' he asked her.

'Not bad,' she said. 'Just one last detail.' She reached out and ripped a small name tag off his chest then flung it aside. 'Just in case we meet somebody who knows the previous owner,' she explained.

It occurred to Kip that Mr Lazarus might be listening in so he announced, a little too loudly, 'This white suit I'm putting on will make a pretty good disguise!'

Kitty gave him an odd look. 'That's the general idea,' she admitted.

'And with the smoked-glass helmet I'm wearing nobody will be able to see my face!' added Kip brightly.

'Did anybody ever tell you, you've a gift for stating the obvious?' asked Kitty. She put on her own helmet and gestured for Kip to follow. She led him across the room, out of the swing door and down the corridor beyond.

Beth stared apprehensively into the gloom, and after a few moments a face leaned forward into the scant rays of light that came from the steel-barred entrance. She relaxed almost instantly as she saw it was a boy, no more than seven or eight years of age; a slight dark-skinned boy with thick black hair and large brown eyes. He was dressed in a T-shirt and jeans but Beth guessed that he was probably a native of these parts. Where had Mr Lazarus told her she was? Ecuador? That was South America, wasn't it?

She remembered that the boy had asked her for food and she shook her head apologetically. 'I don't have anything with me,' she told him. 'I'm sorry.'

The boy shrugged his skinny shoulders. 'Is OK,' he said. 'I was just hoping. They give me nothing to eat since they put me in here yesterday.'

'You speak very good English,' said Beth.

'*Of course he does,*' said a voice in her ear.

'*Remember, this is a movie. Foreigners can always speak good English in these films. Where are you, by the way?*'

'I'm locked in a prison,' muttered Beth, and the boy looked at her strangely.

'*Que?*' he muttered.

'Nothing.' She managed to force a smile. 'My name is Beth.'

'Ramon,' said the boy patting his chest. 'You are American, yes?'

'English,' she corrected him.

'Same thing,' he said.

'Oh, no, it's very different.'

A pause. '*Ask him what he's doing here.*'

'What are you doing here, Ramon?'

'Nothing. I just sit and wait.'

'No, I mean . . . how did you come to be locked up here?'

'Oh, I come over from mainland after wahoo.'

Beth looked at him. 'After what?'

'Wahoo. Is big fish. I know special place by the rocks where they come to feed. On good day I pull in eight, maybe ten fish, feed my family for a month. But this last time I decide to go onto the beach to have my lunch. Men with guns arrive in jeep. They grab me and bring me here.' He spread his hands in a gesture of helplessness. 'What I do wrong? Now I worry, because my parents not know what becomes of me.'

'But they'll know where you came fishing, right?'

Ramon shook his head sadly. 'My father, he make me promise I never come here. He say bad things happen on this island. I think he just make a fuss about nothing and I know the big wahoo are out here so I come anyway.' He rolled his eyes. 'My father was right, yes? This very scary place.'

He glanced up at the sound of a shuffling step on the other side of the bars and Beth saw the big ape man walking by, his shoulders hunched, his long arms hanging almost to the ground.

'What's with *him*?' whispered Beth.

Ramon looked worried. 'I don't know. I think something bad happen to him. I hear that one talking . . .'

'Which one?'

'The man with the big voice . . . very loud, very deep . . .'

Beth, I think he's talking about Doctor Leo Kasabian, the villain of this film!

'He say something about "spearmints" he is making.'

'Spearmints?'

'I think he means experiments.'

'Oh, right...'

'Yes, he say that monkey-man is something he created in the lavatory.'

Despite the seriousness of the situation Beth had to stifle a giggle, 'I think you mean *laboratory*,' she said.

'Yes, lavatory. Place where madmen do bad things with test tubes. I see this in film one time.' He looked wistful for a moment. 'I like very much the movies. You like the movies?'

'I *used* to,' said Beth. 'I'm starting to go off them.'

'Don't be like that, Beth. Listen, I have some very good news for you. Kip is somewhere on the island.'

'You think?'

'I know. He just told me that he's in disguise. He's wearing a white suit with a smoked-glass helmet to hide his face.'

'Oh, well, that'll be handy.'

'You'll soon know him, just look for somebody smaller than everybody else.'

'Yes, but—' She broke off as she realised Ramon was staring at her open-mouthed. 'Who you speak to?' he asked.

'A friend,' said Beth. She looked hopelessly around. 'I suppose there must be some way out of here?'

Ramon shook his head. 'I have good look. These bars they are solid.'

Beth thought for a moment and then she rummaged in her pockets and eventually came out with a hairgrip. She got up from the straw and moved over to the barred door. She reached through, poked the grip into the lock and started fiddling.

'That won't work,' said Ramon dismissively. 'That only work in movies.'

Beth smiled. Ramon was right, of course; she too had seen it done in literally hundreds of films. She also knew that a world the Lazarus Enigma had created would surely conform to all the laws of cinema. Sure enough, after just a short time, there was a sharp click and she was able to push the barred door ajar.

'Wow!' said Ramon, but Beth held a finger to her lips to shush him.

Then she said, very quietly, 'Mr Lazarus, I've managed to unlock the cell door. Now, where's the best place to—?'

'Can't talk now!' hissed the voice in her ear. 'I really have to go!'

'Go?' Beth frowned. 'Go where?' she whispered.

But there was no answer, just a strange whooshing sound followed by silence.

'Weird,' murmured Beth. She turned to look at Ramon. 'OK. Follow me.' And slowly, carefully, she pushed open the cell door and stepped out into the gloom.

CHAPTER THIRTEEN

A Spanner in the Works

Jason Corder sat hunched at the controls of the X Seven stealth jet as it shot low across the shimmering surface of the South Pacific. Every so often his eyes flicked aside to study the screen of the location device, which he had mounted on the control panel. His target was somewhere just off the coast of Ecuador, but the map showed no island in the area where his quarry's red light flashed on and off to indicate his current position.

Corder was simmering – in all his years as a secret agent nobody had ever got the better of him at martial arts, and yet some upstart had managed to come zooming out of nowhere with a black-belt-level flying kick that had sent him tumbling down a flight of stairs like an absolute beginner. Worse still, this mysterious newcomer had managed to bluff his way onto a highly classified secret mission, the very mission that Corder had volunteered for, and had also managed to grab a seat aboard the service's most expensive stealth plane. If word of this ever got out, Corder would be a laughing stock at MI6.

But who was this super agent? Z had said he looked like a kid but, of course, he couldn't be what he actually *appeared* to be; he was too skilled for that. He must be some completely new kind of operative, maybe something the Russians had put together. They'd found a way to literally shrink an agent, make him look like a twelve-year-old kid. There was no other explanation.

Still, Corder was back on track now. He'd be coming up on target soon and, over the time he'd taken to travel here, he had formulated his plan – he'd go in there, hard and fast. He'd find the intruder, eliminate him, eliminate Kasabian, deactivate the Annihilator then get the hell out of there. It was what he'd been doing as long as he could remember and nobody did it better…

Funny that. It had always bothered him that he had no memories of his childhood. It was as though he'd always been a secret agent, as though he'd been born at the age of thirty-four, taking his cocktails stirred not shaken, wearing a black tuxedo and carrying a pistol. He'd often considered booking some time with the resident shrink to talk over the phenomenon, but he never seemed to get round to it. Always too busy saving the world from destruction...

He was just thinking this when the cockpit lit up with an intense white light, and with a suddenness that made him start he realised that an old man was now sitting beside him in the co-pilot's seat, a weird-looking old guy wearing a black fedora hat. Corder was so shocked that for a moment the plane veered dangerously over to one side and he had to make an effort to bring it back on course. When he had done that he returned his attention to the old man, who was sitting there quite calmly and smiling at Corder in a rather weird manner.

'Good day,' he said brightly. 'Mr Corder, I presume?'

Kitty led Kip along a corridor and up a flight of stairs. Occasionally they passed other white-coated men and women, who simply nodded to them as they went by. Kip nodded back, hoping that his ill-fitting costume wouldn't arouse suspicion.

Eventually they came to a glass-fronted door, which they passed through onto a long metal walkway. Gazing down over a steel handrail Kip could see they were overlooking a massive control room that had been carved out of volcanic rock. White-suited workers were moving around down there, checking dials, turning handles and shifting levers. Kip also noticed a strange wiry-looking woman with bright red lips, dressed in a military-style uniform, striding around in the very middle of the room. At her heels shambled a huge ape-like man, his long arms hanging almost to the ground. Kip remembered that Kitty had mentioned these two characters to him when they were down near the secret entrance.

'The control room,' said Kitty's voice, muffled behind her helmet. 'It's from here that Operation Snapple will be initiated.'

'Operation Snapple?' muttered Kip.

'The creation of the rhino sapien army.' She pointed to a huge circular opening at the front of a massive bank of equipment guarded by two armed rhino sapiens. In the mouth of the metal circle restless purple lights flickered and shimmered. 'That's the Kasabian Annihilator. It's from there that

Kasabian's clone army will emerge,' Kitty said. 'In their thousands.' She turned her head towards Kip. 'They're clearly preparing to initiate the cloning process. I think we should go down there and slow things up a little.'

Kip nodded, though he wasn't really sure how they might do such a thing. 'Don't you think we should wait a while?' he asked hopefully.

'Wait for what? Time's ticking away, Jason. Come on.'

Kitty led the way down the metal steps to the control-room floor. She walked straight over to an instrument panel as though she knew what she was doing and turned a dial at random. Then she motioned for Kip to follow her example. He looked around, spotted a metal lever sticking out from a display and gave it a turn to the left. Immediately a red light on the panel began to flash, but within seconds another white-coated worker appeared at Kip's side to push the lever back to its original position. The light stopped flashing. Kip tried flicking off a switch but the same man immediately corrected his action and then wagged a finger at him. Clearly this wasn't going to be as easy as he'd hoped. He looked round for something else he might try to sabotage, but at that moment two more white-suited figures approached him.

'Ah, Professor Olsen,' said a man's voice. 'Just the person we've been looking for. It . . . *is* Professor Olsen, isn't it?'

Kip nodded his head frantically, not wanting to let his voice betray him.

'It's shocking that they couldn't get a suit in your size,' said the man. 'Somebody of your reputation. Bet it wasn't like this in Sweden, eh?'

Kip shook his head. Clearly this Professor Olsen character must be the only other short guy working around here.

'We've encountered a bit of a problem with the nuclear-flux capacitor,' said the other person's voice, a woman. 'We wondered if you could help us out?'

Again Kip nodded. He glanced hopelessly around for Kitty, and realised that with the identical costumes and the smoked-glass helmets he could no longer tell which one she was. The two newcomers had turned away and Kip had no option but to follow them. They walked a short distance across the control-room floor and stopped in front of a huge metal box that was studded with dials, switches and glass displays.

'It seems to be overheating,' said the man's voice, indicating a temperature gauge, the needle of which was seriously close to a red zone. 'We've run all the usual tests, but nothing seems to be working. I don't think it's a serious problem, but we'd like to be sure – and who better than the person who actually designed it?'

Kip looked stupidly around before he realised that the man was actually referring to him – or rather Professor Olsen. He studied the construction for a few moments and told himself that he wouldn't be able to make head nor tail of it if he looked at it for a hundred years. After a lengthy pause he decided he'd better at least *look* like he knew what he was doing, so he reached out and turned a knob that was currently set at number 3 up to number 10. Then he turned a lever from an upright position till it was pointing straight downwards. As a final measure he clicked on two black switches and switched off three red ones. He stood back and waited for everything to go wrong, but suddenly, inexplicably, the temperature gauge began to slide smoothly back down to a safer level.

'Incredible!' said the woman, clapping her gloved hands. 'What a radical approach to the problem!

I'd never have thought of that.'

'Brilliant,' agreed the man. 'Thanks, Professor. It's little wonder they gave you the Nobel Prize.' And he shook Kip's gloved hand before he and the woman walked away.

Kip stood there feeling slightly stunned. He'd had no idea he was a scientific genius. He was just looking around for something else he could mess about with when there was a loud trumpeting fanfare. Everybody stopped what they were doing and turned to stare at a huge screen that came sliding smoothly down from a recess in the ceiling. The screen lit up with the silhouette of the seated man with a cat on his lap – the same image that Kip had seen back in Z's office. Then the deep voice, amplified so much that the room seemed to shake, burst out of unseen speakers.

'My fellow villains! Your attention, please. I have just received the following message from the United Nations.'

The screen flickered momentarily and the silhouette was replaced by a face that Kip instantly recognised – they'd hired a lookalike to play the role, but the man had the same scrubbed-clean, ruddy-cheeked face, horribly appealing eyes and tiny puckered hole of a mouth as the real Prime Minister of Great Britain. He was sitting in what looked like a hotel room. Through a window there was a view of alpine roofs mantled with a thick covering of snow. Oddly, instead of the usual suit, the PM was dressed in what looked like a quilted ski jacket.

'Doctor Kasabian,' he said in that irritating posh voice that Kip knew from a thousand news bulletins. 'My fellow leaders at the UN have elected me to speak to you on their behalf.' He leaned closer to the screen as if to confide a secret. 'I don't mind telling you, it's damned inconvenient. I'm interrupting my family's annual ski holiday. The wife's absolutely livid about it.' He paused for a moment to allow this to sink in before continuing: 'As I'm sure you must be aware, Doctor Kasabian, the world is currently in deep, deep recession. So, we at the UN have had a meeting to decide just exactly what we can spare. Obviously your original demand' – he picked up a piece of paper and smirked at it – 'for a hundred billion dollars is quite out of the question. So we discussed how much we might be able to spare, with every major nation making a contribution, and, after long and exhaustive negotiations, we have arrived at a more realistic figure.' He paused for a moment as though trying to build suspense. 'Doctor Kasabian. We of the United Nations offer you the sum of twenty thousand pounds in cash, plus a year's free membership of my health club... *and* a two week holiday anywhere in the European Union.' The Prime Minister paused and smiled confidently. 'Obviously, you'll want to take a little time to consider our offer, but we feel sure you'll find it acceptable. Remember, this is the twenty-first century and money doesn't grow on trees. Now, if you'll excuse me...' He picked up a couple of ski poles. 'My wife and children are waiting for me out on the piste. My ski instructor reckons I'm a natural.' He headed for the door, walking in a very peculiar fashion, but it was only when he got to the other side of the room that the video camera revealed he was already wearing his skis.

The screen shimmered, and once again Kasabian's silhouette filled the screen. It quickly became apparent that he was not in the best of moods.

'Fools!' he roared. 'Idiots! Do they realise what they've done? They have sealed their own fate. Well, the gloves are off! We shall no longer observe the deadline. Start the countdown procedure with immediate effect. The Kasabian Annihilator will be initiated just as soon as it is ready for launch.' A long pause, then, 'Get on with it!' All the white-suited workers snapped to attention and started busying themselves at their respective bits of machinery. But Kasabian still had one last thing to say. 'Olga! Simeon! Report to me immediately.'

The wiry-looking woman with a face like a bulldog wearing lipstick turned quickly on one heel and started to stride across the control room. The huge apeman shambled after her. Kip glanced quickly around and then noticed that one worker was frantically pulling the arm of another very short person who was gabbling away in what sounded like Swedish.

Kip ran across to intervene. 'Kitty, it's me,' he hissed. He bowed to the other short character, noting the little name tag on his chest as he did. 'Sorry, Professor Olsen, our mistake.' He grabbed Kitty's arm and nodded towards the retreating figures of Olga Katamowski and Simeon. 'We should follow them,' he said. 'They'll lead us to Doctor Kasabian.'

'I had the same idea,' muttered Kitty. 'I wondered why you were pretending to be Swedish.' She bowed her head to Professor Olsen and they turned away to see that Olga was already climbing a staircase at the far side of the room with Simeon bounding up behind her. Kip and Kitty hurried in pursuit.

Beth and Ramon crept slowly and silently along the gloomy hallway, not sure which way they were headed. They came to some more barred cells. The first cell appeared to be empty but then something scuttled forward through the half-light and Beth had to hold back a cry of revulsion as she saw what appeared to be a strange hybrid between a child and a rat scurrying backwards and forward on elongated hind legs, its tiny arms held out in front of it, its pink nose quivering.

'What is it?' whispered Ramon.

'I'd say it's half boy, half rat,' murmured Beth.

'A bat?' offered Ramon, but Beth said nothing and they moved on. In the next cell there was a pink fleshy creature lying on some straw, its flanks rising and falling as it breathed. It looked to Beth's astonished eyes like a pig with a boy's head grafted onto it. She remembered how Dr Kasabian's booming voice had wondered aloud if Beth might be a suitable subject for one of his 'anthropological experiments' and she shuddered at the thought of what might happen to her and Ramon if they didn't make their escape from here.

They moved on along the rows of cages, encountering some new horror in each of them: an eight-legged dog with ten spider-like eyes resting in thick strands of web in the corner of its cage; a horse with a long, spotted neck like a giraffe and four human arms where its legs should be; a huge turtle-like creature with a pale human face peering shyly out from the shadows of its shell. Beth glanced at Ramon and saw that he too was terrified, his big brown eyes moving from left to right in shocked disbelief.

'Who would make such things?' he whispered.

'A madman,' said Beth.

The last cell held the most hideous creature of all: a great olive-green lizard with the arms and hands of a man. It stood unmoving in its cage and occasionally a long purple tongue flicked out from its mouth with a brief swishing sound, snatching up any insects that happened to flutter by. As Beth and Ramon moved past its cage the creature turned its head and fixed Beth with a look of complete misery.

She was happy to see a glass-paneled doorway ahead of them. They paused to peep through it before cautiously pushing it open and stepping into the next section of corridor. From here a flight of metal steps led upwards and Beth started to climb them, keeping her eyes fixed to the way ahead. Ramon followed. The staircase twisted round and went up another level, and they went with it, steeling themselves to flee back down again if anybody appeared from above but, thankfully, nobody did.

They made it to the next level and came to another glass-fronted doorway. Pushing through it, they found themselves on a metal gantry overlooking the big control room that Beth had glimpsed before when she had been hiding in the ventilation duct. Below them dozens of white-suited workers were moving to and fro, checking dials, turning levers. Beth noticed Olga striding up and down in the very centre of the room, slapping her riding-crop impatiently against one of her boots as though eager to conclude some business she had – and she also spotted the strange ape-like man shambling along in Olga's wake, waiting for instructions from her.

Suddenly there was a loud fanfare and all the people stopped work and turned to watch a huge screen that descended from the ceiling. A voice began to boom from unseen speakers, but up where they were Beth couldn't see the screen, or even make out what was being said. She wondered what to do. If they descended the stairs they'd be recognised as outsiders in an instant; but she was also reluctant to go back down the way they had come.

Just then Olga and Simeon started making their way across the control room to another flight of stairs at the far end of it. If Beth had kept watching she might have noticed the two white-suited workers who followed in pursuit of them, one of whom was much shorter than the other; but her attention had just been directed to a row of metal lockers beside her.

Beth reached out and tried the handle of the nearest of them. Inside was a white suit and a smoked-glass helmet, just like the ones that were being worn below. She opened the next locker and found that too had the same equipment inside it.

She dragged out the first suit and began to put it on, keeping herself pressed back against the lockers out of sight. She gestured to Ramon to follow her example and he obeyed, even though both suits were way too big for them and they were obliged to turn back the sleeves and legs. Once they were dressed the two of them looked at each other.

'What we do now?' asked Ramon.

'We need to find somebody,' said Beth. 'A friend. I'm hoping he might be down there somewhere.' She studied the gathering of white-suited workers below her and suddenly noticed one who looked rather different to the rest, a good head and shoulders shorter than the others. Nevertheless, he'd somehow managed to find a set of overalls that fit him perfectly.

Beth smiled, nodded. 'I think that's him,' she told Ramon, pointing. She raised her voice a little. 'Mr Lazarus?' she said. 'Mr Lazarus, it's Beth. I think I've just spotted Kip, right here in the control room. I'm going to go down to try and make contact with him. Mr Lazarus?'

No answer. Beth sighed.

Ramon stared up at her. 'Who you talk to all the time?' he asked.

'Never mind.' She lowered a helmet onto her head and Ramon did the same. Then she turned to study the people below until, once again, she found the one she wanted, the small one who she was now sure must be Kip. 'Come on,' she said. And she led the way down the stairs.

CHAPTER FOURTEEN

Crash

Mr Lazarus sat in the co-pilot's seat looking at Jason Corder. He could hear Beth's voice buzzing in his ear, asking him a question, but he reached into his pocket and switched off her channel so he could concentrate on what he was doing.

Corder was staring back at him as though he couldn't quite believe his eyes. 'Who the hell are you?' he gasped.

'The name's Lazarus. Mr Lazarus.'

'Is that . . . some kind of code name?'

Mr Lazarus considered correcting him but then decided that it would probably be quicker to go along with the idea. 'Yes, it is, as a matter of fact.'

'Aren't you a bit long in the tooth to be doing this kind of work?'

'I don't normally get involved with this side of things. I'm more of a back-room boy. But I've been sent here by . . . er, MI7 to help you with your mission.'

'MI7? Never heard of them!'

'We're new,' Mr Lazarus assured him. 'Still in the early stages of preparation.'

Corder looked far from convinced. 'If you're one of us, you'll have some form of ID with you,' he said.

'Of course.' Mr Lazarus lifted a gloved hand and suddenly a card appeared between his thumb and forefinger. He handed it to Corder, who studied it, puzzled. At first it appeared to be completely blank, but then it shimmered and a succession of moving images appeared on it – a younger Mr Lazarus, dressed in a black tuxedo, was running through a series of explosions and firing a machine gun at some unseen attackers; he was swinging on a rope and holding an attractive female in his other arm; he was performing a death-defying leap from the top of a building into a shimmering blue ocean, thousands of metres below him. He struck the water and disappeared beneath the surface, barely making a splash. Then the card shimmered and was a blank white sheet again.

'Good Lord,' said Corder handing back the card. 'That's some technology you've got there!' He thought for a moment. 'How did you actually *arrive* here? It was as though you just . . . materialised.'

'New techniques,' said Mr Lazarus tapping the side of his nose. 'Department seventeen. Top secret, absolutely hush-hush. We'd hoped to have the equipment ready to send you directly to Doctor Kasabian's hideout but, unfortunately, the kit wasn't tested in time so we had to let you go the old-fashioned route.' He waved a hand at the cockpit's interior. 'But then, when there was a new development, I volunteered to join the mission.'

Corder's eyes narrowed suspiciously. 'What new development?'

'There's been a bit of a mix-up. I believe you're in pursuit of a boy.'

Corder sneered. 'He's *disguised* as a boy. Pretty convincingly too, by all accounts. Convincing enough to bluff his way past one of our top operatives. But it's pretty obvious he's not what he appears to be. For one thing, he beat me at martial arts. Only a highly skilled black belt in Kai Fu could do that.'

Mr Lazarus nodded, as though sympathising. 'I appreciate it must seem pretty fantastic, but I can assure you, he really is just an ordinary twelve-year-old boy who has accidentally found himself in a tricky situation. You see, I was testing out the technology that brought me here...'

'You were testing it . . . on a boy?' gasped Corder. 'Is that legal?'

'Not exactly, but we sail pretty close to the wind in department seventeen. We always try the equipment on children first to, er . . . to keep down costs.'

Corder looked shocked at this news. 'That's . . . outrageous,' he said. 'There ought to be a law against it.'

Mr Lazarus shrugged his shoulders as if to say that such matters were quite beyond his control. 'Anyhow, I was just trying to transport him from our headquarters in London to . . . to . . . the steps of the Tate Gallery. But something went wrong and he ended up in the headquarters of MI6 instead.' He shook his head. 'I've no idea how that happened. As he came flying in he caught you a lucky kick and knocked you down a flight of stairs. An accident, nothing more. Then he panicked and somehow was mistaken for you. So, you see, there's absolutely no reason to harm him . . . or his friend, for that matter.'

'What friend?'

'A girl called Beth. I tested the equipment on her also and . . . well, don't ask me how, but she got sent to Doctor Kasabian's secret hideout.'

'Good grief! Just how many children have you been experimenting on? It sounds like there must have been dozens of them.'

'Oh, no,' Mr Lazarus assured him. 'Just those two. But I wanted to come here in person and tell you that all you need to do is concentrate on your mission. I'll take care of the children.'

Corder looked doubtful. The plane continued to zoom through the sky while he considered. 'I'm not sure,' he murmured. 'How do I know you are who you say you are? You could just as easily be some foreign agent trying to muscle in on my mission. What kind of an accent is that. Italian? You could be with AISE.'

'Who?'

'Don't play the innocent with me, chum. AISE. The Italian Secret Service. They've never forgiven me for that mess-up in Pisa, when I accidentally blew up the leaning tower.'

'You blew up the leaning tower of Pisa?' cried Mr Lazarus.

'Not my fault,' Corder assured him. 'I was aiming the bazooka at a villain but he ducked.' He thought for a moment and then nodded. 'Yeah, that'll be it. The so-called kid is one of your agents who got in a little over his head. I bet that's your game, isn't it? You've developed a squad of super agents disguised as kids, able to zoom in and out of any situation. But this time it went wrong, didn't it? Now I'm wise to your little game and you'll do anything to try and keep it under wraps. Including inventing a story as ridiculous as the one you just told me.'

'But I haven't invented it! I've simply told you what happened. They aren't agents in disguise; they are just children.'

'Yes, and I'm a monkey's uncle.' Corder reached into his jacket and pulled out a gun, which he pointed at Mr Lazarus. 'Now,' he said. 'I want you to hand me the equipment you use to go backwards and forward.'

Mr Lazarus shook his head. 'I wish I could,' he said. 'But I have nothing to give you. The boy has that equipment and I can't go back without it.'

Corder laughed dismissively. 'Oh, right,' he said. 'You're trying to tell me that you'd go into a dangerous mission like this one, with no way of returning to your destination? Why would you do such a thing?'

'Because I feel responsible. I talked Kip and Beth

into doing this and if anything happens to them it will be my fault.'

'Pull the other one, pal, it's got bells on.'

'I'm telling you the truth,' protested Mr Lazarus.

'Don't think I'd hesitate to shoot you,' Corder warned him. 'Just because you're an old man, that doesn't cut you any privileges. I've shot thousands of people without raising an eyebrow and I wouldn't—' He broke off in surprise as a red light on the control panel of the X Seven began to flash on and off making a high-pitched whooping sound. 'Rats!' he snarled.

'What's the problem?' gasped Mr Lazarus.

'Incoming,' said Corder. He pushed the gun into his jacket again and grappled with the steering column, pulling it hard towards him and causing the stealth plane to rise sharply upwards, flinging the two occupants back in their seats.

'In . . . coming . . . what?' gasped Mr Lazarus, struggling with the G-forces that were pulling at his face and body.

'Guided missile,' snarled Corder. 'Didn't realise we were so close to the island. Somebody's launched an attack on us.' He pulled the column hard to the left and the plane swung over with a force that

made Mr Lazarus's stomach lurch. 'Trying to...
throw it off our tail,' hissed Corder. 'But it's...
sticking like glue. Must be a heat-seeker.' Now the
spy thrust the column forward and the plane went
into a nose dive. Mr Lazarus had a horrifying
glimpse of a jungle-covered landscape rushing up
to meet them. Corder left it almost until the last
moment and then leveled out, the palm trees
rushing past the underside of the fuselage in a green
blur.

'I think we made it,' said Corder.

Then there was an impact that shook the plane
like a rat in the grip of a terrier and a terrible heat
blossomed from somewhere behind them. Mr
Lazarus glanced back in alarm and saw the rear of
the plane disintegrating, tumbling backwards into
the air. Corder said something that was lost in the
noise of the explosion and reached out to a lever in
front of him. He pulled it hard, there was a whump
of compressed air and, quite suddenly, the glass
cockpit flew back. Corder's seat shot upwards into
the air and he was gone.

For an instant Mr Lazarus sat, stunned, the air
rushing into his face, the flames behind him eating
along the length of the plane to where he sat. There

was no time to think about his actions. If he did nothing he would be dead in moments. He reached out to a similar-looking lever in front of him and pulled it back hard. There was a click, a *whoosh*, and then he too was being thrust upwards at incredible speed, rising so quickly through the air that he could hardly catch his breath. He caught just a glimpse of the stricken spy plane rushing away below him and then the seat in which he sat reached the end of its trajectory. It span slowly around on itself and began to fall towards the earth.

Just as he was beginning to think that he was done for there was another lurch as a parachute fluttered out from the back of his seat and opened above him. Mr Lazarus began to drift slowly downwards. Half a mile away to his right there was a bright flash of orange as the plane hit the tree line and erupted in a ball of flame. A moment later came the sound of the explosion itself, a dull, booming crash like distant thunder. And then his seat was drifting down through the trees, and Mr Lazarus could see that directly below him was the broad expanse of a glass roof, surrounded on all sides by lush green ferns. He looked up at the chute above him, trying to work out if there was anything he could do to steer the apparatus away from its present course, but there didn't seem to be any way of making such a change and the roof was already dangerously close.

There was nothing for it but to grit his teeth and steel himself for the impact...

Kip and Kitty followed Olga and Simeon up the staircase and along another corridor beyond, keeping a good distance between them and their quarry. Once away from the other workers, Kitty removed her helmet and left it hanging on a convenient hook they passed. Kip took the opportunity to do the same, glad to be out of its suffocating confines. He lifted a hand and brushed his sweaty hair out of his eyes. As they walked along Kitty unzipped her white overall to reveal that beneath it she was wearing a rather racy black leather catsuit. Despite this, she seemed to be as cool as a cucumber. She stepped daintily out of the overalls and left them lying in the corridor like a discarded skin. Once again Kip followed her example, though he wasn't nearly as effortless as she was. As he was attempting to step out of the overalls his foot caught in the garment and he nearly tripped. He had to grab at a length of railing on the wall to steady himself.

He glanced at Kitty but she didn't seem to have noticed anything. She was prowling along like some oversized feline, her gaze fixed intently on the two figures ahead of them. She reached into her catsuit and brought out a deadly looking pistol, the end fitted with a chunky silencer. Kip remembered that he was armed too. He reached into his shoulder holster and attempted to pull out his own gun, but it was held in place by a safety strap and he spent some time fiddling with it before Kitty reached over and skillfully unhooked it for him.

'Thanks,' he whispered. He was surprised by how heavy the gun was. He held it in front of him and noticed that his hand was shaking slightly. 'What do we do when we find Kasabian?' he murmured.

Kitty gave him a puzzled look. 'You know our orders,' she said. 'He's to be eliminated. Whatever else happens, we must succeed. And, remember, no heroics. If anything happens to one of us, the other must go on with the mission.'

'Er . . . right,' said Kip. 'When you say "eliminate", do you mean . . . like . . . actually *kill* him?'

She stared at him. 'Of course that's what I mean! I must say, Triple Zero, I'm surprised to hear you ask a question like that. Your reputation is that of a ruthless killer. That business in Panama... You killed women and children, didn't you? Dozens of them.'

'Oh yeah, well I had to *then*, obviously. They had it coming, didn't they? But, you know... I was just wondering if there was some other way. It's not like Kasabian's doing anything so very bad, is he? He's only, like, creating an army of weird-looking rhino-things.'

'Are you joking? He intends to use that army to enslave the entire world. Millions of innocent people will die!'

'Yeah, if you put it that way, I suppose it would be a bit harsh.'

Kitty looked at him for a moment and then she smiled. 'Oh, I get it. You're fooling with me, right? You do have this reputation for cracking jokes I just didn't realise it would be quite so... over the top.'

Kip shrugged. 'What can I tell you?' he muttered. 'I'm a fun guy.'

Up ahead of them Olga and Simeon turned a corner so Kip and Kitty crept carefully up to it and peeped round. They saw that the two villains had come to a halt in front of a large metal statue of a samurai warrior, his sword raised above his head in a threatening gesture. Olga glanced quickly around as if to ensure that she wasn't being watched. Then she reached up, took hold of the sword and pulled it sharply towards her. There was a click, and the statue divided neatly in half, the edges moving aside to reveal a secret doorway and a flight of steps leading upwards. Olga had a last look around and then went up the steps. Simeon followed. After a few moments the two halves of the statue moved silently back into position.

'Right,' murmured Kitty. She glanced at Kip. 'Ready?' she asked him.

He nodded, though in truth he felt anything but ready. But she was already striding towards the statue and he had little option but to follow her. She reached up a hand, took hold of the sword and pulled it forward. Once again the statue divided. She peered up the steps into the gloom, but from this angle there was nothing to see. 'Come on,' she said. She stepped through the opening and began to climb. Kip reluctantly followed.

The steps led upwards a short distance to a bare

corridor with a stone-flagged floor. Kitty started cautiously forward, her gun held ready, and Kip moved with her. He was aware now of a strident voice coming from somewhere ahead of them – a woman's voice, sounding rather angry. Kip remembered that Kitty had described Olga as having a Russian accent but this voice seemed to have originated in darkest Yorkshire.

'Why do you always fly off the handle like that?' it asked. 'Why must you always lose your temper? You should go back and bargain with them, ask for a better deal.'

The voice that replied was that deep booming baritone, the same voice Kip had heard when he'd watched the broadcasts in Z's office and the control room. 'But they insulted me. Twenty thousand pounds! That wouldn't pay to replace the light bulbs in my secret lair.'

'No, but it were a starting point, weren't it? You could have talked them up, got them to improve on their offer.'

'You don't seem to be listening to me, Mother. They can't be trusted. My defence forces have just reported that they shot down a jet that was intruding into our airspace. Obviously they were sending somebody to eliminate me – a special agent, or something of that kind. How can I do business with somebody so devious?'

'That's just the way they are now. Once upon a time you could trust the good guys to act honourably, but nowadays they're as crooked as we are. Look, why don't we make another film? We'll send it to the UN, saying that if they don't improve their offer we'll order the rhino sapiens to destroy Brussels.'

'Do you think anyone would notice?'

'Well, somewhere more interesting then? Paris, perhaps, or maybe even New York. That would really get their attention. Then maybe we wouldn't have to go to all the trouble of creating millions of clones. A thousand of 'em would cover that job.'

Kitty had reached the open doorway and Kip moved in beside her. He could see Olga standing on the far side of the room talking to a shadowy figure seated in a leather chair. The man still had the white cat in his lap and was stroking it as he spoke.

'Mother, I can't go back on my threat,' he rumbled. 'They'll think I'm weak.'

'But you haven't said anything to them yet.'

'No, but I told my workforce, didn't I? I told them to start the countdown. You can't expect me to tell them to stop now, I'll look like a dufus.'

'All I'm sayin' is—'

That was as far as she got, because Kitty stepped decisively into the room, her pistol out in front of her. 'Hold it right there,' she said. 'Jason, cover me.'

Kip followed her in and glanced quickly around the big circular room. Light was filtering down from a glass ceiling, but shadows still hugged the curved walls and Kip couldn't see the apeman anywhere. He was just thinking this when, without any warning, the creature came leaping down from the light fitting overhead and slammed into Kitty, knocking her off her feet. Her gun went off, spitting a slug uselessly into the nearest wall but she rolled expertly and sprang to her feet, only for a powerful swat from one of the apeman's hands to knock the gun clean out of her grasp.

'Shoot him, Jason!' yelled Kitty, and Kip leveled his gun but somehow couldn't bring himself to pull the trigger. Kitty glared at him then dropped into a martial-arts stance, her hands out in front of her. '*Ah-heh!*' she yelled, and she launched a kick at

Simeon, but he caught her foot in one huge hand and pushed upwards, hard. Kitty went spinning backwards and crashed into a wall. She slumped to the floor with a groan.

Simeon turned and glared at Kip. He started to advance – Kip realised there was nothing for it; he would have to shoot but, in the same instant, he became aware of a gathering darkness that seemed to blot out most of the light coming from above. Quite suddenly there was a crashing sound over-head and broken glass began to rain down all around him. Then something came lurching down through the roof and landed with a heavy thud, catching Simeon a glancing blow and knocking him to the ground in the process. Kip noticed it was some kind of leather seat, the back of it turned to him, so he couldn't see if anybody was actually occupying it and, a few seconds later, a bright orange parachute drifted down through the opening in the roof and covered both Simeon and the seat.

Kip stood there staring in open-mouthed astonishment.

'Jason,' groaned Kitty, clearly too stunned to stand. 'Get him. Get Kasabian!'

Kip nodded dumbly. He stepped quickly round

the parachute-covered heap in the middle of the room and lifted the pistol to point it at the figure in the chair.

'No,' whispered Olga, 'Please, don't!' Her accent was still Yorkshire.

Kip ignored her. His finger tightened on the trigger, but in the same instant the figure in the chair leaned forward into the light and gazed at his would-be killer with appealing blue eyes. Kip stared back and his mouth dropped open once again. He was staring at what appeared to be a nine-year-old boy, a boy with blond hair and an angelic-looking face. He had a device strapped around his head with a microphone attached to it and some kind of gizmo that must have been used to change the tone of his voice, but it was a kid sure enough, a kid who was now smiling triumphantly as he sensed Kip's bewilderment. Kip also noticed one last detail. The cat the boy had on his lap wasn't real. It was one of those toys that used batteries to make it look as though it was breathing.

'It's not my fault,' boomed the deep, deep voice. 'I'm allergic to real cats.'

'Kill him!' gasped Kitty from somewhere behind Kip.

'But . . . he's just a—'

Then something struck Kip hard across the shoulders and he dropped the gun and went reeling across the room. He crashed against the far wall and slid down it, stunned. He saw that Olga had just swatted him with her riding crop. She bent over and picked up his dropped pistol, then came towards him, the weapon raised, a cold smile on her lipstick-encrusted mouth.

'So,' she murmured. 'You came to kill my boy, did you?' Kip noted that the Russian accent had mysteriously reappeared. 'But it's not Leo who will die today, my friend. It's you.' And she tilted back her head and laughed: a deep, unpleasant laugh that seemed to fill the entire room.

Kip's hand was already under his T-shirt, grabbing the retriever and flipping open the cover with his thumb. He knew that Mr Lazarus had warned him it was dangerous to do this, but what other choice did he have? He was dimly aware of Kitty struggling to her feet, of Simeon coming out from the cover of the parachute and moving to intercept her.

'Jason!' cried Kitty despairingly as the apeman grabbed her, pinning her to the wall.

'Time to die,' said Olga, and she pulled the trigger in the same instant that Kip's thumb pressed the eject button.

Then the powerful light was blazing in Kip's eyes and his flesh felt as though it was melting. He heard the thud of the bullet being fired and the dull crunch as it slammed into the wall behind him. But it seemed a hundred miles away, and he was falling, falling into the white light . . . And then, quite suddenly, he was sliding backwards, into the more familiar surroundings of the projection room. He half fell, half staggered off the wooden platform.

'That was close,' he said. 'I nearly got . . .'

He looked around. The film was still running, clattering through the projector, but there was no sign of Mr Lazarus anywhere. Kip looked around and scratched his head – then remembered what the old man had said to him the last time they'd spoken. He'd said he was coming into the film.

'Oh great,' muttered Kip. He remembered the leather seat that had parachuted into the room and the way he'd wondered if anybody was actually sitting in it. He moved across to the viewing hatch and stared through it at the big screen in the auditorium, hoping to see what was happening in

Kasabian's hideaway. But the scene had changed. Now there was Jason Corder trudging through a jungle and looking far from pleased.

CHAPTER FIFTEEN

Mistaken Identity

Jason Corder *was* far from pleased. As he trudged, sweating, along the narrow jungle trail, the events of the last half hour or so kept playing through his mind on an endless loop. He couldn't believe that he, the world's top spy, had messed up so completely. He'd lost concentration for a moment back there and allowed himself to be shot down by enemy forces like some absolute beginner. It wasn't really his fault, he told himself; he'd been distracted by the sudden appearance of the weird old guy in the fedora hat. But exactly who was he? How had he managed to magic his way into the cockpit like that? And, most importantly, which side was he on?

One thing was for sure. Corder needed to win back a little respect, and the best way to do that was to crack on with his mission. He would find Dr Kasabian and liquidate him, quickly and ruthlessly – and anybody else who got in his way, be they man, child or old-age pensioner, was going to have to pay the same price. There would be no more Mr Nice Guy from here on.

Corder emerged into a clearing and saw the ground slope steeply away from him into a lush river valley. About halfway down the slope a brick hatch stuck up clear of the undergrowth. He made his way towards it, placing his feet with care, not wanting to stumble. When he finally got to the hatch he was surprised to see that a steel grille, which had originally covered the opening, had been swung to one side as though somebody else had recently passed this way. He clambered up onto the hatch and peered down into the gloom, noting the series of metal rungs set into the stone wall of the shaft. A gust of stale air rose from below, ruffling his hair. A ventilation duct, he decided, and a sure way into Kasabian's hideaway.

Corder shrugged off his torn and stained jacket and flung it to one side. He pulled the pistol from its shoulder holster and checked that it was loaded and in full working order. Returning the gun to its holster, he lowered himself into the shaft until his feet connected with one of the metal rungs. Then he began to descend, quickly and urgently, into the bowels of the earth.

Beth led Ramon down the stairs, taking in the wide expanse of the laboratory as she did so. In the very centre of the room she could see a huge circular opening that was flashing with multi-coloured light. On either side of it stood two heavy grey figures that could only have been the result of one of Kasabian's mad cloning experiments. They were holding guns and looked like they meant business – but Beth made her way directly towards the short figure in the white suit who, as they approached, was pretending to be busy at a control panel, turning levers and clicking switches as though he actually knew what he was doing.

Beth stepped up beside him and leaned in close to talk to him. 'Surprise, surprise!' she said.

He stopped doing what he was doing and turned his head in her direction. 'Who are you?' asked a muffled voice; and Beth reminded herself that because of the smoked-glass helmet she was wearing, Kip couldn't see her face.

'Who do you *think* I am?' she cried. 'It's me. Beth!'

'Beth? Beth who?' The muffled voice seemed to have some kind of foreign accent and Beth started to realise that she might have made a terrible mistake.

'Oh . . . er . . . it's—'

'Is it Elizabeth?' asked the voice. 'Doctor Elizabeth Templeton?'

'Er . . . yeah . . . yeah that's right!' Beth nodded frantically. 'Sorry, didn't mean to disturb you, I'll let you get on with your . . . your stuff.' She started to turn away.

'No, wait.' The man's hand shot out and grabbed her arm. 'What a coincidence,' he said. 'I was just thinking about you. There's something here you can help me with . . .' He seemed to become aware of Ramon standing there, looking at him. 'Who's this?' he asked. 'Oh, wait, let me guess. You're even shorter than me so it can only be . . . Professor Kam Kai Dang, yes? From Vietnam?'

'Er . . . yes,' squeaked Ramon, nodding frantically.

'Nice to meet you, Professor. Loved your article on genetically enhanced crops in *New Scientist*! Particularly what you were doing with rice. You understand what I'm saying?'

'Yes, yes!' squeaked Ramon.

'These outfits are ridiculous, are they not? I cannot understand why we are obliged to wear them; they make communication so difficult. And these ID badges are too small, don't you think? Through the smoked visor you can hardly make them out. And you know how bad my eyesight is.' He indicated a name tag on his breast that read *Professor Lars Olsen*.

'They're no use at all,' said Beth slapping a hand over her own name tag. She glanced at Ramon and saw that his tag read *Dr Edward Baxter*, but Professor Olsen didn't seem to have noticed anything amiss. He turned back to the control panel. 'Now, Elizabeth, you see the pressure indicators there?'

'Uh huh.' Beth pretended to be listening but she was frantically gesturing to Ramon to cover up his name tag. After a few moments he caught on and slapped a gloved hand over it, so loudly that Professor Olsen actually turned to look at him.

'Can you see all right, Professor Kai Dang?'

'Yes, thank you,' said Ramon, nodding.

'Good. Now, here's my question: why are these indicators fluctuating all the time? You see how they are flickering?'

'Umm.' Beth stared at the gauges for a moment. 'That would be ... because ...'

'Yes?'

'Because they're ... faulty?'

'Oh, no, they have been thoroughly checked, only this morning. I made sure of that. I was wondering if there could be some kind of natural oscillation occurring – perhaps a type of hyper-extendable micro-oscillation? Caused by the fact that we're counting down a little earlier than expected.'

'You're ... counting down?' croaked Beth.

'To Operation Snapple, yes. Didn't you know?'

'Er ... no, I ...'

'Did you not hear Doctor Kasabian's order earlier? We were told to proceed with the creation of the clone army as soon as possible.'

'Umm ... I ... must have missed that.'

'So, what do you think?'

'I think it's really *dumb*. I've never liked clowns at the best of times, but a whole army of them running round, throwing custard pies at people—'

'Not clowns, Elizabeth, *clones*!'

'Oh, clones, right. Yeah, that's fine with me. I'm not fussed on clones either, but if the doc thinks they'd be useful, why not? I expect they'd come in handy. This place could do with a good clean, for starters.'

'Elizabeth, I'm talking about the fluctuation! Do you think it could have been caused by the premature countdown? Obviously we're using Lake Boasian as the primary energy source, but there was supposed to be a longer build-up to the release. Could that be affecting things?'

'It . . . it could,' agreed Beth. 'Oh, yes, I think so.' She looked at Ramon. 'What do you think, er . . . Professor?'

'Yes,' said Ramon nodding like a maniac. 'Yes, that is what it is, for sure! The fructilation! It's been caused by the premier mountdown!' But Ramon was nodding too hard. The helmet, already much too big for him and not properly secured at the neck, came loose and fell to the floor with a heavy clunk. Ramon stood there staring open-mouthed at Professor Olsen, one hand clutched to his chest to hide his name tag.

'You're not Professor Kam Kai Dang,' said Professor Olsen.

'Oh, no, silly me. I got mixed up,' Beth tried. That's Professor . . . Edward Baxter from . . . from the University of . . . Venezuela!'

'But he's a *child*,' said Dr Olsen coldly.

'I know, incredible, isn't it? He's the youngest professor in history. He's in *Guinness World Records*, and everything.'

But now Professor Olsen reached out and moved Beth's hand to reveal *her* name tag. He leaned closer to peer at it. 'And according to this, you are . . . Doctor William Fairbrother.'

'Oh, yeah . . . my suit's in the wash, I borrowed this from a friend.'

It was no use. Professor Olsen reached up his hands, took hold of Beth's helmet and wrenched it off.

Because of the smoked-glass visor he still wore she could only imagine what his expression must be like, but she supposed it wasn't very pleasant.

'Who *are* you?' snarled Professor Olsen. 'Who sent you here?'

Beth glanced around quickly. Other white-suited workers were realising that something was amiss and they were advancing on her and Ramon. Somebody must have hit an alarm because lights began to flash and a siren wailed. The two rhino-like creatures by the big flashing circle were also moving closer, their guns raised.

Beth and Ramon began to back away as the white-suited horde came after them.

'Now don't get excited,' Beth told them. 'There's a perfectly good explanation for all this. You see, I was at the pictures watching this film and—'

Her shoulders came up against something immovable – the hard wall of a ventilation duct. A short distance to her left there was a metal grille, and she wondered if she had time to prise it open and jump inside – but even as she was thinking it, there was a sudden crash from within and the grille flew outwards and clattered to the floor. A familiar face appeared at the opening, gazing cold-eyed at the gathering of workers in front of him.

'Daniel!' cried Beth, and the secret agent paused a moment to give her an odd look. 'I mean, *Jason!*' she corrected herself.

'Do I know you?' he muttered.

Beth was about to explain that they hadn't actually met in person but she'd seen every one of his movies, but she didn't have time because that was when Corder went into action, leaping out from the opening, gun blazing. He stopped six white-suited workers in their tracks. Then, his gun empty, he slipped into a fighting stance. The first rhino sapien came lurching at him, gun raised to fire, but Corder performed a nimble somersault and lashed two feet into its face, sending it crashing backwards into its companion. The creatures went down in a heap and before they could even think about rising, two swift blows were delivered to their heads and they were out for the count. As Corder straightened up Professor Olsen aimed a punch at him but he deflected it easily, hit the professor with a blow to the stomach and, as he doubled over, a knee to the head that smashed the glass visor on his helmet and flung him head over heels onto the ground. There was a brief pause, and then all the remaining white-suited figures came running at Corder in a vengeful mass. He seemed to turn into a human whirlwind, his arms and legs flying in all directions as he unleashed the full fury of his Kai Fu moves, flinging his opponents around him like straw dolls.

'Wow!' murmured Ramon, staring in astonishment at the carnage. 'Who's *he*?'

Beth gave a deep sigh. 'He's my hero,' she said.

Olga Katamowski lifted the folds of the parachute silk to reveal an old man in a black fedora, sitting in what looked like a pilot's seat. She leveled her gun at him. 'Who the hell are you?' she snarled.

'Pleased to meet you,' said Mr Lazarus. 'And I would ask you not to say that word, it's very impolite. You must be Olga, I've heard all about *you*.' He extended a gloved hand for her to shake but she recoiled from it as though he was armed.

'Stand up,' she commanded. 'And keep your hands in full view.'

'No problem.' He got carefully up from the seat and looked around. 'Lovely place you have here,' he said. He gestured at the shattered roof. 'Sorry about the damage. Though, to be honest, secret hideaways like this one do tend to get destroyed sooner or later.' He stepped away from the seat, wincing at the sound of glass crunching under his Italian leather shoes. 'So sorry to drop in unannounced but ... well, it's been an unusual sort of day.' He took another look around the room, noting the big ape-like man who was struggling to keep an attractive young woman in a leather catsuit under control, and the young boy who was crouched against a wall studying it intently as though looking for something.

'Where did he go?' asked the boy, speaking in the

deep, booming voice that Mr Lazarus recognised from Dr Leo Kasabian's transmission. 'He just seemed to dematerialise an instant before the bullet hit him.' The boy lifted a hand to trace a small hole in the wall with the tips of his fingers.

'*You're* Doctor Kasabian?' asked Mr Lazarus stepping forward.

'Stay where you are,' demanded Olga, but he ignored the order.

'Yes,' growled the boy, turning to look up; and Mr Lazarus could see the headset he was wearing to distort his voice. 'And who are you?'

'My name is Mr Lazarus. I'm really sorry for staring in such a fashion but, I must say, I expected somebody a little . . . older.'

'They all say that,' boomed Kasabian. 'It's not easy being an evil genius when you're only nine. That's why I usually allow myself only to be seen in silhouette.'

'Fascinating,' said Mr Lazarus. 'It's quite an achievement for one so young. Now, who did you say dematerialised?'

'Another boy, perhaps a few years older than me. A boy with dark hair. My mother tried to shoot him and he just . . . vanished.'

Mr Lazarus sighed, realising that he must have missed Kip by a few seconds.

'That was no boy!' cried the young woman, who was still struggling desperately to escape from the clutches of the ape-like man. 'That was my partner!'

Mr Lazarus looked at her. 'No,' he assured her. 'He wasn't. I'm sorry, I don't believe I know your name . . .'

'It's Kitty,' said the woman, and she stopped struggling. 'Kitty Velour.'

'Kitty! What a delightful name. Now, I realise you *think* it was Jason Corder . . .'

'Jason Corder?' cried Olga. 'The famous spy? That . . . child?'

Mr Lazarus shook his head. 'I understand your confusion,' he said. 'I'm afraid it's all become horribly mixed up. That was just a friend of mine, a boy called Kip, who has somehow been mistaken for Mr Corder.' He looked meaningfully around. 'One mistake has led to another and he's now totally out of his depth and, to some degree, I have to admit, it's all my fault.' He thought for a moment and then raised his voice. 'But hopefully, he'll be coming back pretty soon. He's got our only means of escape, hasn't he? And there really isn't a lot of time left...'

Kasabian stared at him. 'What are you on about?' he muttered. 'Who are you?'

'That really doesn't matter,' Mr Lazarus assured him.

'It matters to me,' boomed Dr Kasabian walking towards him. 'Tell me what you're doing here. What's your mission?'

Mr Lazarus glared at him. 'I'm sorry,' he said. 'It's hard to take you seriously when you sound like that.' He reached out a hand and yanked one of the wires connected to Kasabian's microphone, pulling it free.

'Don't touch that!' cried Kasabian, but his voice was suddenly reduced to a brattish squeak that sounded every bit as Yorkshire as his mother. He looked at Olga. 'Mum, he's pulled me microphone out! Shoot him!'

'Just a moment, dear. Let's find out what he wants first.' She now seemed to have abandoned all pretence of being Russian.

Mr Lazarus spread his hands in a gesture of helplessness. 'I don't really *want* anything. I came here to get the boy...'

'To *get* the boy?' cried Olga. 'You mean, to liquidate him?'

'Oh, no, just to take him home. Him and his friend.' He looked at Kitty again. 'I don't suppose you've seen another young person? A girl, name of Beth, dark hair, about the same age as the boy who disappeared?'

Kitty shook her mane of auburn curls.

'There *was* a girl like that,' muttered Olga. 'We had her thrown in the cells. She was barmy. Said she was on her way to Benidorm—'

'I don't understand,' interrupted Kitty. 'The boy pretended he *was* Corder.'

'Yes, well, he probably didn't want to disappoint you. You know what kids are like.'

She seemed to consider for a moment. 'No,' Kitty said. 'I've no idea what they're like. In fact, now you mention it, I think your boy was the first I've ever met—'

'Oh, yes, of course,' said Mr Lazarus, remembering that movie characters had no memories of previous experiences since they'd rarely ever had any. 'In your line of work you probably don't have much time to—'

'Just a minute,' snarled Olga. 'What exactly is

going on here? My son and I are trying to bring about the end of the world as we know it and you're just complicating things.'

'I appreciate it must be very annoying,' admitted Mr Lazarus. 'But I really will get out of your hair, just as soon as I—'

'My hair? What's wrong with me hair?' asked Olga, and she lifted a hand to touch her blonde tresses. 'I was supposed to be getting it done this afternoon.'

'Oh, no, that's just a figure of speech. Your hair is quite . . . charming. Now, why don't you go on with what you were doing? I really don't want to spoil things for you.'

But Kasabian didn't seem happy with this response. He stared at Mr Lazarus. 'You don't seem bothered,' he muttered.

'I beg your pardon?'

'My mother just told you we're trying to end the world and you didn't even lift an eyebrow. Aren't you *scared*?'

Mr Lazarus shrugged his shoulders. 'Not particularly,' he said.

'Why not?'

'Well, it's just that I know something you don't know.'

'Which is?'

'You won't actually manage to do it. Oh, you'll come very close, the seconds will be counting down to zero, but at the last moment the hero will come in and save the world.'

Kasabian threw back his head and laughed. 'I'd like to see somebody try.' He walked across the room until he reached the doors of a metal cabinet. He opened it to reveal a huge digital clock, which was counting down the seconds. The clock currently read nine minutes and twenty-three seconds. 'As you can see, the countdown to Operation Snapple has already begun,' said Kasabian. 'The mechanism can only be deactivated in this room and nobody else knows how to find it.'

'Even so,' said Mr Lazarus, 'a hero will come and—'

'You're not listening!' snapped Kasabian. 'The only way to deactivate the Annihilator is to enter an eleven-letter code, so even if you were to start trying to guess it now you'd never be able to work it out.'

Olga cocked the pistol and pushed it into Mr Lazarus's back. 'Not that we're going to let you try,' she added.

Mr Lazarus lifted his hands. 'Oh, don't worry about *me*; I have no interest in stopping you.' He glanced across at Kitty. 'I've no doubt she'd like to have a go, but in situations like this the female characters rarely get a chance to show what they can do; they usually turn into helpless victims . . . And, besides, it's quite clear that the large gentleman there isn't going to allow her to move . . .' He returned his attention to Kasabian. 'What's his story, by the way?'

'Simeon's one of my early experiments,' the boy said proudly. 'I spliced his genes with those of an African silverback gorilla, and that's the result. He's quite obedient, but he does cost me a fortune in bananas.'

'I see. Why?'

'Because I have to get them shipped over from the mainland and—'

'No, I mean, why did you do it?'

Kasabian looked troubled. 'Because . . . well, you probably wouldn't be interested.'

'We've a little while before the hero arrives,' said Mr Lazarus. 'And it *is* traditional in these situations for the villain to outline his motivation, so why not fill the time usefully?'

'Very well.' Leo Kasabian looked wistful. He took a few steps forward until he was standing in the direct glare of an overhead spotlight and then he began. 'From an early age, I knew I was a genius,' he said. 'At nursery school, when the other kids were doing "Baa Baa Black Sheep", I was reading the sonnets of Shakespeare...and correcting the grammar. At the age of six I left school because they could no longer teach me anything. At seven my social-networking site, Flunge, made me the world's youngest multimillionaire...'

'*Flunge?*' murmured Mr Lazarus.

'It's changed its name since then,' murmured Olga. 'Now it's called F—'

'Mother!' Kasabian stared balefully at Olga. 'You're interrupting my flow. Now, where was I . . . ? Ah, yes! I began to despair that anything would ever interest me again. But one day I discovered the work of the famous anthropologist, Franz Boas, and I knew I had discovered my life's obsession.' Kasabian pointed to a huge marble bust of a man's head standing on a plinth in the corner of the room. 'Using Boasian techniques I began to experiment with gene splicing. My first attempt was fairly primitive. I created a sprog...a cross between a sparrow and a frog!'

'Cute little thing,' whispered Olga. 'We called him Mr Croaky.'

Kasabian ignored her. 'For my next attempt I was more ambitious. I gave the world a camster – a cross between a camel and a hamster. It was an incredible achievement but I couldn't find a wheel big enough for it to exercise in, so it put on weight and died.' He looked sad for a moment, before continuing. 'The world's scientists mocked my research, but I was inspired! Of course, they didn't understand, they never would. The stupid fools! I realised I needed a place where I could hide from the world, a place where I could conduct my experiments in total secret. I came here and had this laboratory built over a huge pool of molten lava which I named in honour of my hero.' He gestured once again at the marble bust. 'I continued with my work, creating many other creatures before, finally, I achieved perfection with my rhino sapiens.' He frowned. 'But even my immense wealth was beginning to run out. I needed more money in order to continue with my research. So I hatched a plan to hold the world to ransom, telling the leaders that if they did not meet my demands I would create a vast army of rhino sapiens and unleash them. If my demands had been met we could have avoided any unpleasantness. But the fools have refused to pay me the money – so now they will have to pay the ultimate price... They must lose everything, everything they ever believed in.' He smiled at Mr Lazarus. 'So... that's me, in a nutshell,' he said. He looked at Olga. 'I think that would have sounded better with the deep voice,' he added.

'It was very nice, dear,' said Olga.

Mr Lazarus smiled. 'That's quite a story,' he said. 'And I *do* sympathise.'

'Sympathise? With what?'

'With the fact that it simply isn't going to work out for you. You see, it's the hero's job to save the world, and I happen to know that he's already here on the island.'

Kitty brightened. 'Jason's here? The *real* Jason?'

'Yes, my dear... He's nothing like as pleasant as Kip, but, on the other hand, he is an expert spy and I'm sure he'll be along in a moment to sort things out.'

'No he won't!' cried Kasabian marching up and down and stamping his feet. 'That wouldn't be fair.

Me and Mum have worked really, really hard on this and I'm not going to let some rotten secret agent come here and spoil everything!'

'Calm down, dear,' said Olga.

'I will not! Who does he think he is?' Kasabian cried pointing at Mr Lazarus. 'Why has he come here to try and wreck my plan? I think you should shoot him!'

'Not just yet,' said Olga. 'We may need to use him as a hostage.'

'Oh, yes, I suppose you've got a point.' Kasabian strode back to Mr Lazarus and stared up into his eyes. 'In exactly...' He glanced at the countdown clock. 'In exactly six minutes and nineteen seconds the Kasabian Annihilator will have amassed the necessary power to begin creating my clone army. And there's nothing that anybody can do to stop it!'

Back in the projection room Kip was standing with one foot on the wooden platform, staring through the hatch at the screen. There was Mr Lazarus; there were Kitty, Olga and Simeon; and there was some kid who was claiming to be the film's evil villain. Right next to them a clock was ticking away the final minutes before the Kasabian Annihalator began to create its mutant army. Kip knew it was incredibly dangerous, but he had to get back into the movie now. He could grab Mr Lazarus and the two of them could get out of there, but what about Beth?

There was no time to ponder the matter. Kip took a deep breath and launched himself forward into the light – but, even as he pushed off, he was aware of the scene just changing on the big screen. It was too late to stop anything: the light was in his eyes, his body was melting and he was falling, falling...

CHAPTER SIXTEEN

Hero

Jason Corder turned away from the heap of white-suited villains who were scattered across the floor in front of him and came towards Beth and Ramon, his fists raised.

'Whoah!' cried Beth. 'Steady, Jason. We're on your side, remember?'

Corder relaxed a little, as it occurred to him that Beth had greeted him when he'd first arrived. 'All right,' he said lowering his hands. 'Now, perhaps you'd like to start by telling me who you are.'

'I'm Beth,' said Beth brightly. 'Beth Slater. And this is my friend, Ramon.' She smiled. 'Thank goodness you came along when you did, we were in a tight corner.'

'And how is it you know me, when I've never laid eyes on you before?'

'Oh, because I've seen all of your fi—' Beth frantically tried to change tack. ' . . . Your files. Yes,

I've read your MI6 files. I'm a big fan. I loved the flying-dragon punch you did on that last guy,' she added. 'You used that in *Diamonds Are Expensive*, didn't you?'

'What are you jabbering about?' snarled Corder. He thrust an index finger at Ramon. 'Is this the kid who's been impersonating me?' he asked.

'Oh, no, you're thinking of my other friend, Kip. Ramon's just a local fisherboy. He came here after the wahoo.'

'The what?'

'It's a kind of fish.'

'Never mind about that nonsense. Where's Kasabian?'

'I'm not sure,' admitted Beth. 'He's supposed to have some kind of a secret hideout around here, but nobody seems to know exactly where it is.'

'Don't lie to me,' snapped Corder. He glanced up and noticed that all around the control room were big displays indicating a digital countdown that was now on five minutes and fourteen seconds. 'My God!' he whispered. 'Has it begun? Has it actually begun?'

'I'm afraid so,' said Beth, and held out her hands in a 'what can you do' sort of way.

Corder snapped back round to glare at her. 'Where's Kasabian?' he asked again.

'I honestly don't know,' Beth assured him. 'I'd tell you if I did.'

Corder didn't hesitate. He grabbed hold of Ramon, spun him to face Beth and, in one lithe movement, pulled a deadly looking knife from his jacket, which he held to the boy's throat. 'You'd better speak up,' he said, his voice expressionless.

Beth stared at him in dismay. 'I'm telling you the truth,' she told him. 'Please, you have to believe me.'

'Why should I? You're here in the control room, you're dressed the same as Kasabian's other people, and you seem to know more about me than you should.'

'But you don't understand, I—'

'Listen, I'm going to count to three, and if you haven't told me where Kasabian is, the kid is history. Do you understand?'

'Please, you can't—'

'One!'

'And I thought you were so nice!'

'Two!'

'Jason, please!!'

'Thr—' A blinding white light filled the room, and suddenly something came whizzing through the air at astonishing speed. A pair of Converse trainers hit Corder full in the face and catapulted him backwards across the room. The deadly knife clattered onto the floor as the special agent smacked against a metal control panel and then crumpled slowly to the floor, unconscious.

Kip's bottom connected with the ground and he let out a yell. He lay for a moment grimacing with pain, then sat up and registered that the unconscious figure sprawled on the ground in front of him was Jason Corder. 'Not again,' he groaned.

'Kip!' Beth ran over and helped him to get up. Then she threw her arms around him and gave him a fierce hug. 'You saved us!' she cried.

'I did?' Kip looked blearily about and registered Ramon. 'Who's he?' he asked.

'His name's Ramon. He's a local fisherboy. Corder was just about to cut his throat.'

Kip looked again at the crumpled figure of Jason Corder. 'But I don't understand. I thought he was the good guy.'

'So did I, but he turned out to be horrible in the flesh.'

Now Kip was staring up at the countdown on all the screens. 'We're nearly out of time,' he said.

Beth nodded.

'Then we've got to wake up Jason Corder! He's supposed to save the world.' He kneeled down beside the spy and shook him roughly but he was out cold. He looked up at Beth. 'Aren't you going to help me?' he pleaded.

'No way, he's a nasty piece of work!'

'Well then, we've got to get to Mr Lazarus.'

'He . . . he's in the film?'

'Yes, he came in to try and rescue us.'

'I thought he'd gone a bit quiet.'

'As usual, it all went wrong. Now he's being held captive in Doctor Kasabian's secret hideaway. I was trying to get to him but the scene must have changed just as I was coming in.'

'Well, don't sound so fed up about it! At least you found *me*.'

'I'm not fed up, but the countdown's started and Kasabian's hideaway is the only place where it can be stopped.'

'But . . . nobody knows where that is.'

'Actually, I do. Come on, follow me.' Kip turned and started running for the metal staircase up which he and Kitty had followed Olga and Simeon earlier. Beth and Ramon had no option but to run along after him, pulling off their white overalls as they went.

'I don't understand,' cried Beth. 'How can you possibly know where it is?'

'I've been there before,' he said.

'You have? When?'

'About ten minutes ago.'

They reached the stairs and Kip pounded up them, aware as he did so that the digital displays around the control room now read four minutes and fourteen seconds.

'You've been out of the film and you came back? Mr Lazarus said you weren't supposed to do that!'

'I know, but I had to. I was about to be shot.'

'Oh . . . so what's the big hurry to get back there?'

'Don't you get it? Corder was supposed to save the world, but I've just knocked him out. If we don't do it, this world, the world within the film will be destroyed. And if we're still here when that happens, I reckon we'll be stuck here for ever.'

'Then we should leave now.'

'We can't, not without Mr Lazarus.'

'Oh,' said Beth. 'Yes, I suppose that makes sense...'

Ramon had been looking from one to the other of them as if following a tennis match. 'What are you two talking about?' he cried. 'Why you keep mentioning films?'

'It's complicated,' said Kip. 'And there isn't time to explain.' They reached the top of the stairs and pounded along the corridor beyond. 'It's just along here,' he said. 'Oh, and, Beth?'

'Yes.'

'As we're going, try to think of some eleven-letter words. We might need them.'

'What?'

'I was watching on the screen just before I came in. Kasabian said that the countdown could only be stopped if you entered an eleven-letter word. You're good at puzzles and things.'

'Yes, but—'

'Just get thinking!'

With the last minutes ticking away they ran down the corridor towards the statue of the samurai.

★★★

They waited in the secret hideaway: Mr Lazarus, with Olga's gun pointed between his shoulder blades, and Kitty, her wrists still held in Simeon's powerful grip. Meanwhile Dr Leo Kasabian was strolling up and down still talking about his favourite subject – himself.

'Of course, I'm not really a doctor,' he admitted. 'I just used that title because people always expect an evil villain to have some kind of formal training.'

Mr Lazarus nodded. 'I'll take a wild guess and say that Leo Kasabian is not your real name, either,' he said.

Kasabian brought his hands together in a burst of mocking applause. 'Very good,' he said. 'But don't bother asking me what it is because I'm not going to tell you, no matter how much you beg.'

'It's Reggie,' said Olga. 'Reggie Sparks. I think it's a lovely name.'

'Mum!' snarled Reggie. 'Did you have to tell him that?'

'Don't worry, dear, we'll be shooting him in a minute or two.'

Mr Lazarus smiled. 'I take it Olga Katamowski isn't *your* birth name, either?'

She nodded. 'Gladys Sparks, at your service. I've nothing against our real names but Reggie insisted that we change them. It was the same with that daft Russian accent he had me do. He kept saying that no real villain ever came from Barnsley.'

'He obviously has a flair for the dramatic,' said Mr Lazarus. 'And he's brilliant for his age. I would, however, like to ask one more question. It's about your master plan.'

'What about it?' asked Reggie.

'You're planning to create a clone army to enslave the world, correct?'

Reggie nodded.

'And this machine you've built, the Kasabian . . .?'

'Annihilator. Yes, yes, well?'

'It seems to me you'll need an incredible source of power to run such a machine.'

Reggie and Gladys exchanged a look and then both burst out laughing.

'Yes,' agreed Reggie.

'But . . . no conventional energy supply could give you the kind of power you'd need for such a huge task.'

'Not to mention the gigantic electricity bill,' added Gladys.

'Exactly. So how will you . . . ?'

Reggie sneered. 'In case you haven't noticed, we're sitting on top of one of the most powerful energy reserves in the world,' he said.

'Are we?' Mr Lazarus looked at the carpeted floor beneath him. 'I really don't . . . Ah, I think I understand. The volcano!'

'Exactly!' Reggie grinned delightedly. 'When I built this place I recognised its potential straightaway. I have harnessed the power of an underground lake of molten lava to run everything here – but I'm using only a fraction of what's available. There's enough power in the lake to keep the Annihilator running for a hundred years if necessary. I'll be able to create an army of billions. I'll be king of the world.'

'And I'll be queen,' said Gladys.

Reggie gave her a look. 'Technically, you'll be more like a duchess,' he said. 'But you'll be rich beyond your wildest dreams.'

Mr Lazarus shook his head. 'Ah, but you're both forgetting something. Any moment now Jason Corder will come running though that door to put a stop to this countdown.'

'I don't think so. There's only three and a half minutes to go.'

'Even so. I'm familiar with these situations. You'll see.'

'Forget it. Even if Corder arrived here now there's absolutely nothing he could...' Reggie broke off at the sound of footsteps thudding along the corridor outside. Everybody turned to gaze at the open doorway.

'Jason!' cried Kitty.

And then Kip ran into the room, followed by Beth and Ramon.

'Ha!' cried Reggie. 'Three kids. So much for that idea!'

'Hold it!' yelled Kip. He lifted a hand and they all saw that he was holding what looked like a ballpoint pen. 'Throw down your weapons or I'll use this,' he said.

'A pen?' cried Reggie. 'What are you going to do, write us a nasty letter?'

'It may look like an ordinary pen but when I press the button three times...' Kip did exactly that before throwing the device into the middle of the room. 'Hit the floor!' he yelled, and Beth and Ramon did as he said, but everybody else just stood there staring at the pen, which lay on the carpet doing nothing at all. Kip looked up and noticed that it wasn't flashing red like it was supposed to. That was when he realised that Z had somehow managed to give him the wrong pen. 'Oh, crap,' he said. He got wearily back to his feet.

'What was that all about?' asked Reggie.

Kip could only shrug his shoulders. 'It was supposed to explode.' He glanced apologetically at his friends. 'Sorry,' he muttered.

'Mother, get him!' snarled Reggie.

Gladys pushed Reggie aside and came striding towards Kip, her gun raised. Kip thought about using the watch, but didn't feel right about cutting a woman in half with a laser beam. Just at that moment, he remembered something else and fumbled in his pocket. His fingers connected with a small black cube the size of a matchbox.

'Put your hands in the air!' said Gladys, pointing the gun. Kip did as he was told, the black cube in one hand and he moved the slider with his thumb as he did so. Then, as Gladys stepped up to him, he reached slightly forward and dropped it down the front of her shirt. For an instant, absolutely nothing happened. She just stared at him in bewilderment. Then, quite suddenly, the front of her shirt ballooned as the tent began to inflate.

'Blinking Nora!' she exclaimed, an instant before a metal stake came flying up from under her collar and smacked her on the chin, stopping her in her tracks. Simeon let go of Kitty and moved to help Gladys, but Kitty took the opportunity to unleash a flying kick into the back of the apeman's head and he collapsed face down beside his mistress. Kitty then turned towards Kip but, as she did, another stake came flying out of Gladys's ruined shirt and clouted the agent on the forehead, knocking her to the floor. There was a wild flapping of canvas and then there was a large tent where Gladys used to be.

Kip recovered himself and stood looking warily around the room at the other people still standing – Mr Lazarus, Reggie, Beth and Ramon.

'I'm not exactly sure what you did there,' said Mr Lazarus. 'But I have to say it was pretty spectacular.'

'Thanks,' said Kip. 'We secret agents have our little tricks, you know.'

Reggie brought his hands together in another burst of mocking applause. 'Nicely done,' he said. 'But you're way too late.' He indicated the face of the clock, which was now on one minute and twenty-three seconds. 'You can't stop the count-down,' he said.

Kip approached it and saw that there was a small keyboard below the screen. He glanced at Beth. 'Any ideas?' he asked her. 'Because if not...' He pulled the Retriever from under his T-shirt and beckoned to Mr Lazarus to come closer.

But Beth shook her head. 'We can't just let him win,' she said. 'That's not the way these things are supposed to end.'

'We only have forty-four seconds,' Mr Lazarus reminded her.

Beth looked at him and then at Reggie. 'Eleven letters,' she murmured. 'I wonder...' She reached over to the keyboard and typed in LEOKASABIAN. Everyone looked expectantly at the clock but the countdown continued.

'You must think I'm an idiot!' laughed Reggie. 'As if I'd be that obvious!'

'Thirty-two seconds,' said Mr Lazarus.

Beth thought for a few more moments and then typed in NAIBASAKOEL

Wrong again.

'Pathetic,' laughed Reggie. 'My name backwards! Hah! You must think I'm a complete amateur.'

'Twenty-three seconds.'

Kip grabbed Beth's arm and motioned to Mr

Lazarus to hang onto him. He flipped open the case of the Retriever and the red light pulsed beneath his thumb. 'We have to go!' he urged her.

'No wait a moment,' she said. She thought for what seemed the longest time. 'Maybe it's an *anagram*,' she murmured. She glanced at Reggie and saw his expression falter. Then she glanced quickly around the room and her gaze fell on the bust of Franz Boas standing on its plinth; and that kicked up a recent memory in her brain, a memory of when she was about to cross the lake of molten lava. There had been a sign beside the lake, hadn't there? But what exactly had it said? She remembered, checked the letters in her mind. They seemed to fit. She glanced quickly at the counter. It was down to twelve seconds and there was only time for one last attempt. She took a deep breath and typed in LAKEBOASIAN.

And the counter stopped – with four seconds to go.

Chapter Seventeen

Plan B

There was a long deep silence. Reggie stared at the clock in disbelief. Then, 'What have you done?' he whispered.

Beth grinned proudly. 'What does it look like?' she asked. 'I've stopped the countdown, haven't I?'

Kip clapped her on the back. 'That's brilliant!' he cried. 'Beth, how did you work it out?'

'I remembered something I saw earlier,' she said. 'When I was underground.'

'You . . . you mean you *cheated*!' cried Reggie.

'I didn't cheat,' protested Beth. 'I just have a good memory.'

'To be fair,' said Kip, 'she's always been very good at puzzles.'

Reggie started to march up and down, his hands on his hips, stamping his feet. 'It's so not fair!' he protested. 'It's a dirty rotten trick. How could you possibly . . .?' He broke off as a low rumble made the entire room shudder. Kip noticed that all the colour drained instantly from Reggie's pudgy little face. 'Oh, no,' he murmured and his voice was full of dread. 'Oh, that's great!'

The shaking in the room seemed to be getting worse. 'What's happening?' asked Kip uneasily.

'The volcano,' whispered Reggie. 'I harnessed the energy of Lake Boasian in order to power the Annihilator.'

'So?'

'So now that power has nowhere to go.'

'What does that mean?' asked Beth.

Reggie glared at them. 'Have you ever heard of Krakatoa?' he asked.

'I think I had it in a Chinese restaurant once,' said Kip, trying to be helpful.

'No, you idiot! Krakatoa was a volcanic island in Indonesia. In eighteen eighty-three it exploded with the force of two hundred metatons of TNT. Forty thousand people were killed.'

'Er... why are you telling us this?' asked Kip.

'Because I have a terrible feeling that history may be about to repeat itself,' said Reggie. He turned quickly away and walked over to where Simeon was lying. 'Wake up!' he yelled, launching a kick into the giant's ribs. 'Don't just lie there, you idiot, there's work to be done!'

Simeon stirred and lifted a heavy browed head to look up at his employer. He gave a low, snuffling grunt.

'Get up and find Mother,' instructed Reggie pointing at the tent. 'She'll be in under that lot somewhere. When you find her put her in the cupboard.'

Simeon grunted again but dragged himself obediently to his feet. He shuffled over to the tent and began to tear up the nylon covering with his bare hands, ripping the fabric like sheets of tissue paper. Eventually he found Gladys lying at the bottom of it, her shirt in rags round her. He lifted her up and swung her over his shoulder as though she weighed no more than a towel. Then he started carrying her to the far side of the room.

Reggie meanwhile had found the stuffed cat and was cramming it down the front of his jacket.

'What are you doing?' Kip asked him.

'Well, you can stay here if you like,' said Reggie, 'but now your smarty-pants friend there has put the mockers on everything, we're getting in the cupboard.'

'The *cupboard*?' murmured Beth.

'Yes. I'd invite you to join us but there's only room for three in there, and Simeon already takes up more than his fair share.' He turned and began to follow the apeman who was shambling to the other end of the room. Then he seemed to remember something and he hurried back to get the marble bust of Franz Boas, catching it just as it fell off its plinth. The bust was so heavy he struggled to carry it, but he turned and staggered after Simeon as best he could.

'Wait a minute!' cried Kip. 'You can't just hide in a cupboard. There must be something you can do to stop the island from exploding.'

Reggie shook his head. 'Nope. Not now you've interrupted the countdown. It was something I didn't plan on.' He looked sadly around his head-quarters. 'It's a real shame,' he said. 'I had everything fixed up lovely here. I was going to put in a pool table in the spring.'

Simeon had now reached what looked like a tall larder with a heavy swing door. He turned the handle and flung it open, then climbed inside taking Gladys with him.

Reggie was going to go in after him. That was when Kip picked up the gun that Gladys had dropped. 'Stay right where you are!' he demanded.

Reggie turned and looked back at him. He rolled his eyes. 'You're not going to shoot me,' he said. 'Let's face it, you're not the type. You've done a good job, all of you but, at the end of the day, you're just dumb kids. If you want my advice I'd get off this island as quickly as possible . . . That's if you really do want to live to spy another day.' He winked at Kip and then stepped in through the opening, slamming the door behind him. There was a brief silence, followed by a deep rumble . . . but it was not like the previous ones. This seemed to come from the base of the larder. Smoke and flame began to belch out of the bottom of it and then, with a sudden whoosh of air and a flash of light, the whole thing launched itself upwards and smashed through what was left of the glass roof. In seconds it was no more than a tiny dot zooming up through the stratosphere.

'Well I never,' said Mr Lazarus. 'An escape pod. How ingenious.' He turned to look at his companions and nodded at the Retriever, which hung on its length of chain around Kip's neck. 'Well, I think now it really *is* time we got out of here.'

But Beth was gazing thoughtfully at Ramon – and Kip had just remembered that Kitty was still lying slumped on the floor unconscious.

'We can't go yet,' he said, aware as he did so that the ground beneath his feet was now shaking violently. 'We have to try and get our friends to safety.'

'I doubt there's time,' Mr Lazarus told him sternly. 'And, besides,' he stepped closer, 'they're only fictional friends.'

'That doesn't matter,' said Beth. 'We can't just leave them here. We need to find them a way off this island.'

Ramon beamed. 'My boat!' he cried. 'We use my boat!'

Beth looked at him. 'Where is it?' she asked.

'It should be where I left it, pulled up on the beach.'

'Can we get to it in time?'

'I think so.'

'Then let's go,' said Kip. He ran over to Kitty and shook her back to consciousness. 'Wake up, Kitty!' he yelled. 'We have to get out of here!' She moaned and opened her eyes. He managed to get her to her feet by putting a shoulder under her arm.

'Jemima Kensington?' muttered Beth and there was a certain edge to her voice.

'Er... no, this is just Kitty. She's er... my contact.'

'Your what?'

'Never mind,' said Mr Lazarus. 'If you two insist on doing this, then we need to get moving. But I don't even know how to find a way out of here.'

'I do,' said Beth. 'Follow me.' She turned and led the way towards the door, and the others followed her.

As Kip passed through the doorway, helping Kitty along, he glanced back and saw that items in the room were beginning to fall to the floor. Books rained down from shelves. The countdown clock shattered. The marble plinth on which the bust of Franz Boas had stood tipped sideways and smashed to smithereens.

They ran out into the hallway, which appeared to be vibrating so rapidly that the details were a blur. Clouds of dust sifted from overhead making them cough. They hurried along the length of the corridor and went down the metal staircase beyond. Kip could feel it lurching and swaying under his feet, threatening to tip him over the rail at any moment.

They made it to the control room – only to be confronted by a bruised, swaying figure who was staring at them in baffled rage.

'Jason!' cried Beth.

'You!' cried Triple Zero, pointing an accusing finger at her. 'And you!' he added as Kip reached the bottom of the stairs. 'Why, you little demon, you knocked me out again!' He took a threatening step forward, but Kitty was coming back to full consciousness now and she stepped forward to confront him.

'Not a good time,' she said taking Corder's hand. 'I'm Kitty Velour.' She fluttered her eyelashes. 'I'm your contact here.' The two of them stood for a moment gazing into each other's eyes.

'Corder. Jason Corder. Nice to make your acquaintance.'

'You're everything I expected,' she murmured.

'And you're beautiful,' he replied.

'Oh, for goodness sake!' cried Beth, 'Can you please save all that rubbish for later? This place is going to explode at any moment.'

'But I have to find Kasabian!' protested Corder. 'I have my orders to think about.'

'Forget your orders,' Kitty said. 'We'll never catch

him now, unless you happen to have a rocket in your pocket?'

'Come on!' yelled Beth, and she led the way across the control room, picking through the piles of white-suited figures scattered across the floor. They reached the ventilation duct, the metal grille still hanging open from where Corder had made his entry a short while earlier. Beth scrambled through the opening and the others followed one by one, with Kip bringing up the rear. They began to crawl on hands and knees along the smooth, metal tunnel, clattering and shaking around them.

'I'm too old for this!' complained Mr Lazarus, his voice echoing along the tunnel. 'Can't we just use the Retriever?'

'Not yet!' Beth yelled over her shoulder. 'Everyone keep moving, it's not too far.'

Sure enough, after a few frantic minutes, they reached the point where the ventilation shaft angled upwards. Beth grabbed hold of a rung and began to climb. The others followed her.

Bringing up the rear, Kip heard a grinding noise behind him and glanced over his shoulder, only to see a whole section of duct crumple like a plastic cup squeezed in a giant's fist. 'Hurry!' he urged the others.

It was finally his turn to climb and he pulled himself upwards, just as the section of tunnel he was in was flattened by some prodigious power.

Beth got to the surface and pulled herself out, then turned back to help Mr Lazarus and the others. One by one they got free of the shaft. As Kip reached up to take Beth's hand, he was suddenly aware of a terrible heat blossoming below him. He made a last frantic scramble and rolled off the lip of the opening; at which point a column of flame shot upwards just behind him, rising some six metres into the air.

'That was close!' gasped Corder. He looked at Kip as though impressed by his moves. 'Who *are* you?' he asked. 'How is it I've never met you before?'

'The name's McCall. Kip McCall,' said Kip, realising as he did so that he'd always wanted to say it like that.

'There's no time!' Beth reminded them. She pointed to the hill that rose up ahead of them, and they could all see that huge cracks were forming in the ground as though an incredible pressure was building somewhere down below. 'This place is going to blow apart very soon!' she announced. She looked at Ramon. 'The boat?'

Ramon looked up to the sky, shielding his eyes with the flat of one hand as though trying to get his bearings. Then he pointed at the hill. 'This way!' he cried and began to run up the steep slope.

The others followed, Kip and Beth helping Mr Lazarus, who really *was* too old for this kind of thing. Kip noticed that Corder was now helping Kitty, one arm around her slim waist. *Typical*, he thought.

'I can't go on,' gasped Mr Lazarus. 'I'm pooped. We'll have to use the Retriever!'

'Not till we know the others are safe,' Kip insisted.

'But they're fictional!' protested Mr Lazarus.

'Not to us,' Beth assured him.

They continued to climb, veering round the opening cracks in the ground, in some cases jumping over them. They finally reached the top of the hill and Ramon led them to the left for quite a distance before descending the far side of the ridge and heading down towards the sea. Sure enough, there, in a secluded cove, a small fishing boat was waiting on the sand. The fisherboy ran down the hill and Corder and Kitty went after him. Kip noticed that the two of them were now hand in hand, running together as though they were partners.

Kip and Beth slowed down and Mr Lazarus strove to regain his breath. Ramon paused and glanced back at them, a questioning look on his face, but they waved him onwards.

'We'll catch you up!' yelled Kip. Then he looked at the others and nodded. He flipped open the cover of the Retriever with his thumb. 'I think they'll make it now,' he said.

Even as he spoke he could feel the earth shuddering beneath his feet and hear a strange continuous noise from somewhere far below them, building slowly from a muted growl to an earth-shattering roar. Clearly there was no time to waste.

'Grab hold!' he urged them. Beth threw her arms around his waist and Mr Lazarus threw his arms around Beth's shoulders. Kip flipped back the covering and pressed the button. For an instant nothing happened. Kip was horribly aware of the ground beneath him exploding apart in a great flare of orange heat. And then white light filled his eyes, his body began to melt, and he was falling...

CHAPTER EIGHTEEN

Sunday Matinee

The wooden platform slid backwards and they tumbled from it into the reassuring ordinariness of Mr Lazarus's room, the film still clattering noisily through the projector. They lay there for a moment getting their breath back. Kip was aware of a burning smell and, glancing down, he saw that the soles of his best Converse boots were partially melted. It was going to be fun explaining that one away. He glanced at Beth and Mr Lazarus. 'You two OK?' he asked.

They nodded. Everybody got slowly, painfully, back to their feet – then quickened at the sounds that were coming from the auditorium.

Kip moved to the window and looked through at the image on the screen. He could see Ramon, Corder and Kitty heading out to sea in the little fishing boat. Ramon, in the stern, had just started his outboard motor and it was moving quickly away from the shore.

There wasn't room for all three of them to see through the hatch so Kip moved to the door, unlocked it and went out into the auditorium. Beth and Mr Lazarus joined him. They found themselves seats about halfway down and sank into them to see how it all panned out. They were looking at a long shot of the island with the boat in the foreground racing towards the camera. Suddenly the island behind their new friends erupted in a huge explosion. A close-up showed Corder and Kitty gazing back, the light of the explosion reflected momentarily in their eyes. Then there was a long shot of a huge wave rising from the shores of the island and heading out to sea; a shot of Ramon struggling to keep the boat on course, his dark face scowling. Now the tiny boat was being lifted by the wave and was sweeping along the top of it like a brightly coloured cork. For a moment it seemed as though the tiny craft would be engulfed but, somehow, it managed to stay afloat. The waves gradually subsided and the boat continued to putter away across the blue sea, while behind it a column of fire and smoke belched up against the perfect turquoise sky.

The camera moved in for another close-up of Corder and Kitty. He had his arm round her again and she was staring into his eyes as though they had known each other for ever.

'What a floozy,' muttered Beth. 'They only met five minutes ago.'

'Jealous?' asked Kip slyly.

'No way! What a nasty piece of work he turned out to be. Besides...' She looked at Kip. 'My boyfriend beat him in a fight. Twice.'

Kip smiled. While they hadn't exactly been fair fights he couldn't help feeling incredibly pleased with himself. 'I suppose I did,' he admitted.

'Well,' murmured Corder up on the screen. 'Looks like that's one more mission that's gone with a bang.'

Kitty fluttered her eyes again. 'I'd say you're owed a vacation.'

'Why don't we start right now?' said Corder, and they kissed.

'Uh-oh,' said Kip. 'Cheese alert!'

The music began and the female singer began to croon her awful theme song. The title credits rolled, and Kip reflected how he had, once again, come so very close to being a permanent fixture in a movie.

'Well,' said Mr Lazarus, 'that all seemed to go smoothly enough.'

Kip and Beth stared at him in disbelief.

'You are joking,' said Kip. 'That was a disaster from start to finish.'

'Oh, I wouldn't say that. I think we all learned some valuable lessons there.' The old man looked at them as though expecting a response but they just continued to stare at him accusingly. 'Anyway,' he continued, 'next time, you'll be better.'

'Next time?' muttered Kip. But even he had to admit that he didn't sound quite as appalled as he might have.

'That's a wrap,' said Mr Lazarus. He was about to get up from his seat but seemed to remember something. 'Kip? Haven't you got something for me?' he asked.

'Huh? Oh, yeah . . .' Kip reached into his jeans pocket and pulled out the ID. He glanced at it for a moment and then handed it across to Mr Lazarus. 'I hope it was worth all the trouble,' he said. He unslung the Retriever from around his neck and handed that over too.

'Oh, I'm sure it was . . . and I think I'd better take that fancy watch of yours for safe-keeping,' added Mr Lazarus. 'We don't want any accidents, do we?'

'Aww,' said Kip, but Mr Lazarus wasn't about to be denied.

'Come on, Kip, that's more money to get this place fixed up.'

Kip sighed, but reluctantly unstrapped it and handed it over.

'Excellent,' said Mr Lazarus, slipping it into his pocket. 'My collector friend will be delighted. And just think...thanks to you and Beth the Paramount can now have the steam-clean treatment your father wanted. I'll get onto it first thing tomorrow.'

As if on cue somebody climbed the steps from the foyer into the auditorium. It was Dad and he had Rose with him. He stood there staring at them.

'Hey, come on, you two. What's the idea of sitting around in here? We've got a Sunday matinee to run. The kids'll be arriving any minute now.'

'I'll go and get the film cued up,' said Mr Lazarus slipping the ID card into his jacket pocket. Kip and Beth got up from their seats and went to join Mr McCall.

'What film were you watching?' he asked them.

'*Spy Another Day*,' said Kip.

'Oh right, I didn't realise that had already arrived. Any good?'

'It was . . . different,' said Beth.

Dad waggled his eyebrows at her. 'How was Daniel Crag? I believe you're a big fan.'

'Not any more,' said Beth. 'Actually, I think it's time he retired. I know somebody who'd be *much* better in the role.' She glanced meaningfully at Kip and he felt himself colouring up, but Dad didn't seem to notice anything.

'Well, Beth, do you want to give me a hand to check the auditorium? Kip, you and Rose can go and get started on the popcorn.'

'OK, Dad.' Kip went down the stairs to the foyer and Rose walked alongside him, looking at him intently.

'What are you staring at?' he asked.

'I'm wondering how you managed to get so dirty just watching a film,' she said.

Kip looked down at himself and saw that his sister was absolutely right. His jeans were caked with dirt and grease, and his T-shirt was torn in several places. Now he thought of it, Beth was in an even worse state, her best dress and tights torn to rags. Dad never noticed that kind of thing, but he'd have to be sure to go straight to the bathroom when he got back home or Mum would have some difficult questions for him.

'It was a pretty intense film,' he said as though that explained everything. 'It was . . . almost like you were in it, if you know what I mean.'

He opened the door of the office and went through it into the confectionery booth. He switched on the popcorn maker and upended a large bag of corn kernels into it. Then he started feeding cans of pop into the empty slots at the back of the drinks chiller.

Rose continued to gaze at him. 'There's something going on,' she said at last.

'Don't be silly,' he said. 'Of course there isn't.' But he couldn't look at her.

'There's something about Mr Lazarus and that funny machine he put in here . . . I don't know what it is but there's something weird. And I'm going to find out what it is.'

There was a long silence. Kip stood there trying to think of something to say – but, at that moment, the swing doors of the entrance burst open and a crowd of yelling kids came running into the foyer – and, at the same time, the first golden buds of popcorn began to tumble from the popcorn maker into the heated glass container, filling the booth with a mouth-watering aroma.

Kip let out a sigh of pure relief. 'Show time!' he said. And he hurried into the office to sell the first ticket.

NIGHT ON TERROR ISLAND

PHILIP CAVENEY

It's the scariest movie ever and they're stuck in it!

Have you ever wanted to be in the movies? Kip has, and when he meets mysterious Mr Lazarus he thinks his dream's come true because Mr Lazarus can project people into movies. Films like Terror Island, full of hungry sabre-toothed tigers and killer Neanderthals.

When Kip's in a film, everything is real: real bullets, real swords, real monsters. But he must beware . . . if he doesn't get out by the time the closing credits roll, he'll be trapped in the film forever! Can Kip rescue his sister before the sabre-toothed tigers get her? And if he can – how is he going to get back?!

9781849392709 £5.99

THE ISLAND OF THIEVES

JOSH LACEY

Buried treasure. Ruthless gangsters. An ancient clue . . .

Our Captayne took the pinnace ashore and I went with hym and six men also, who were sworne by God to be secret in al they saw. Here we buried five chests filled with gold.

Tom Trelawney was looking for excitement. Now he's found it. With his eccentric Uncle Harvey, he's travelling to South America on a quest for hidden gold. But Uncle Harvey has some dangerous enemies and they want the treasure too. Who will be the first to uncover the secrets of the mysterious island?

Praise for other books by this author:

'A delight'
The Times

'Smart and pacy'
Sunday Times

9781849392457 £5.99

WILL GALLOWS

& THE SNAKE-BELLIED TROLL

DEREK KEILTY

ILLUSTRATED BY JONNY DUDDLE

It's time for revenge!

Will Gallows, a young elfling sky cowboy, is riding out on a dangerous quest. His mission? To bring Noose Wormworx, the evil snake-bellied troll, to justice. Noose is wanted for the murder of Will's pa, and Will won't stop until he's got revenge!

'Wow, what a brilliant read. Fresh and original – and very funny too. This cowboy's riding to an exciting new frontier in fiction.'
Joseph Delaney, author of *The Spook's Apprentice*

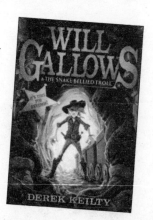

9781849392365 £5.99

A TALE
DARK
AND
GRIMM

ADAM GIDWITZ

Reader: beware!

Lurking within these covers are sorcerers with dark spells, hunters with deadly aim and a baker with an oven big enough to cook children in. But if you dare, pick up this book and find out the true story of Hansel and Gretel – the story behind (and beyond) the breadcrumbs, the edible house and the outwitted witch. Come on in. It may be frightening, it's certainly bloody, and it's definitely not for the faint of heart, but unlike those other fairy tales you know, this one is true.

'Gidwitz balances the grisly violence of the original Grimms' fairy tales with a wonderful sense of humour and narrative voice. Check it out!'
Rick Riordan

'*A Tale Dark & Grimm* holds up to multiple readings, like the classic I think it will turn out to be.'
New York Times

9781849393706 £5.99

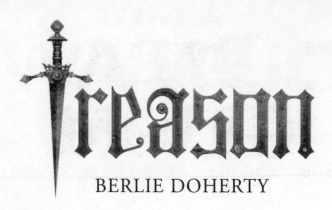

Treason

BERLIE DOHERTY

Who matters most? Your father or your king?

Will Montague is a page to Prince Edward, son of
King Henry VIII. As the King's favourite, Will gains
many enemies in Court. His enemies convince the
King that Will's father has committed treason and he is
thrown into Newgate Prison. Will flees Hampton
Court and goes into hiding in the back streets of
London. Lost and in mortal danger, he is rescued by a
poor boy, Nick Drew. Together they must brave
imprisonment and death as they embark on a great
adventure to set Will's father free.

'Doherty paints a very vivid
picture . . . almost Shardlake for
young readers.'
Independent on Sunday

'A beautifully paced and measured
story. 5 stars.'
Books for Keeps

9781849391214 £5.99

OUTLAW

Stephen Davies

The rules are there to be broken

Fifteen-year-old Jake Knight is an explorer and
adventurer at heart but this often gets him into trouble.
When a stuffy English boarding school suspends him
for rule-breaking, Jake flies out to Burkina Faso where
his parents are living. He is expecting a long,
adventure-filled vacation under a smiling African sun.
But what awaits him there is kidnapping, terrorism and
Yakuuba Sor – the most wanted outlaw in the Sahara
desert.

'A strong desert setting and a corkscrew of a plot make
this a terrific page-turner.'
Julia Eccleshare, LoveReading4Kids

'Stephen Davies writes brilliantly'
Writeaway

'Exceptional talent'
The School Librarian

9781849390880 £5.99

HACKING
TIMBUKTU

STEPHEN DAVIES

Long ago in the ancient city of Timbuktu, a student pulled off the most daring heist in African history – the theft of 100 million pounds worth of gold. It was never recovered but now a cryptic map of its whereabouts has been discovered.

Danny Temple is a good traceur and a great computer hacker. When the map falls into his hands and he finds himself pursued by a bizarre group calling itself *The Knights of Akonio Dolo*, both of these skills are tested to the limit. From the streets of London to the sands of Timbuktu, this high-tech gold rush does not let up for a moment.

9781842708842   £5.99